SAVAGE CARROT

SAVAGE CARROT

INGRID TOMEY

CHARLES SCRIBNER'S SONS • NEW YORK
Maxwell Macmillan International • Toronto
Maxwell Macmillan International
NewYork • Oxford • Singapore • Sydney

Charles Scribner's Sons Books for Young Readers
Macmillan Publishing Company
866 Third Avenue
New York, NY 10022

Maxwell Macmillan Canada, Inc.
1200 Eglinton Avenue East
Suite 200
Don Mills, Ontario M3C 3N1

Macmillan Publishing Company is part of the Maxwell Communication
Group of Companies.

First edition
Printed in the United States of America
10   9   8   7   6   5   4   3   2   1

Library of Congress Cataloging-in-Publication Data
Tomey, Ingrid.
Savage Carrot / Ingrid Tomey.
p.   cm.
Summary: Thirteen-year-old Carrot tries to come to terms with the sudden
death of her father and the family's new life on her grandmother's farm.
ISBN 0-684-19633-6
[1. Death—Fiction.   2. Grief—Fiction.   3. Family problems—Fiction.
4. Farm life—Fiction.]   I. Title.
PZ7.T5844Sav 1993
[Fic]—dc20   93-7273

To Paul,
the celestial, and my soul's idol

For those who helped, for those who encouraged, I offer grateful acknowledgment: Lori Durbin, "the chicken lady," without whose generous advice there would have been no chickens or eggs; Cheryl Tapp and all the instructors at the Walled Lake Outdoor Center, who showed me the world again through the eyes of a child; the wonderful members of Detroit Women Writers, especially Bettie Cannon, whose beautiful *A Bellsong for Sarah Raines* became my bellsong. And finally, thank you to Clare Costello, an editor of wisdom, clarity, and understanding.

SAVAGE CARROT

1

*C*arrot hung upside down in the chair beside the fireplace, her hair falling to the braided rug. Her bare legs stuck straight up like two white posts, but her sneakered feet turned in the air in worried circles. She was looking at the moose. Squinting, she studied his great broad nose with its drooped-over nostrils and the long black mouth hanging sorrowfully over his jaw. Even from below, she could see one of his marble eyes glistening in the light from the kitchen. As if it were full of tears.

"Moose," she whispered, "why do you look so sad?"

From the kitchen end of the big room she could smell onions cooking, hear cupboard doors banging, and she knew she should get up and help Gram. She lifted her head and felt the blood pounding in her temples. Her eyes felt tight, like they were going to pop out on the floor. "Uhhh," she groaned, lying back down and closing her eyes. She would not think of Gram, or the moose, or anything at all.

"Carrie Turvy—your face is as red as your hair. You're going to get a nosebleed, sleeping upside down."

Carrot opened her eyes and looked up at her sister. Upside down, Beaut reminded her of a mermaid with her long yellow hair falling over her bare shoulders.

"I wasn't asleep," Carrot said. But it came out, "I wadden ah sleeb," like she had a cold. She sat up and felt the blood rush back down from her head to her heart to her veins. She blinked several times to clear her head and then she stared at Beaut who was wearing her orange bikini. "Cripes, Beaut—it's only May first."

"I need to work on my tan. I heard there are cheerleading tryouts in three weeks."

"Cheerleading? You don't waste a second, do you?"

Beaut put her hand out to Carrot and pulled her up. "I've wasted a whole month and so have you."

Carrot clung to Beaut's hand in the unlighted living room. She looked around at the huge old piney room, at the saggy green sofa against the far wall where six windows gave a view of the drive stretching away into the deep woods. She looked at the faded plaid chairs beside the mantel and the fireplace that crept up to the squat ceiling, darkened from years of smoke and hundreds of knotholes. And, as if she had never seen it before, she looked at the moose head. With its great expanse of antlers lifting like two opened hands, it seemed to be asking for something. For what? She looked up at Beaut, at her calm, pretty face, and squeezed her hand. But instead of asking about the moose, she said, "Where's Mom?"

"She's doing her hair," Beaut said. "C'mon." She let go of Carrot's hand and led the way to the lighted end of the room where Gram was draining a kettle of potatoes over the sink.

2

"So there you are," Gram said, without looking around. She reached up in the cupboard for the plates, and her long gray braid came tumbling out of its pins. She shook it out straight so that it swung over her broad shoulder when she turned around with the plates. "One of you set these out and the other go see about our Babe. He's not back yet, or if he is back he's lost his way from the shed to the front door."

Suddenly Beaut became unsure of herself. "Would you go?" she whispered to Carrot. "I wouldn't know how to find him." But just then Babe came in the back door, babbling about the chickens as if there were someone beside him.

Babe wore a plaid sport coat and red bow tie, but in spite of Gram's best efforts he never looked very businesslike. Today he had chicken feathers in his dark hair and, as usual, he brought in the smell of chicken poop. It didn't matter to Carrot.

"Hi, Babe," she said, smiling back at her uncle as he waved both his big arms at her, like she was standing half an acre away in the cornfield. She automatically moved toward Babe to sit next to him, then hesitated. Putting her hands on the back of the chair she took a deep breath, squinting at the chinks and dents in the dark wood of the table. It wasn't like before, when she always knew where to sit—all four of them laughing and passing the silverware along without even thinking about it. Now the table seemed too big, with too many chairs. She looked at Gram.

"Over here, Carrot," Gram said, scraping back the chair next to her and motioning for Carrot to sit. "And you, sit

3

yourself across from me," she said, pointing to Beaut, who stood buttoning a green sweater over her bathing suit. "And now, my dears, we shall eat as soon as your mother gets here."

"She's—" Beaut looked quickly over her shoulder in the direction of the stairway. "She said to start without her."

"No, we shall not," Gram said, folding her hands and settling back in her chair.

She said it cheerfully enough but Carrot knew she meant what she said. Carrot wouldn't go get her. She would just make things worse. She looked at Beaut.

"I'll go," Beaut said, rising quickly.

Babe took advantage of the lull in the conversation to start talking about the chickens again. "Tomorrow," he said, patting the table with both hands in an anxious rhythm. "Tomorrow Henny Penny hatches her chicks. Tomorrow is twenty-one days and fifteen baby chicks. Henny Penny wanted to peck my hand off tonight, Mama."

"If you keep piddle-paddling around her nest, you'll make her give it up, Babe. Best to leave her alone."

"But I can't wait. Can't wait. Can't wait." He beat the rhythm with his fat hands on either side of his plate. "Carrot, can you can't wait neither to see Henny Penny's chicks?"

Just then Beaut came back downstairs with their mother. "Here we are," she said cheerfully. "Doesn't Mom look pretty?" Like Beaut she had long blond hair, and Carrot noticed that she had pinned it up loosely and stuck little fake violets across the top so that she looked like an old-fashioned advertisement for something like face cream or English Breakfast tea.

"I'm afraid I truly can't eat a bite," her mother said, snugging up the deep collar of her satin robe, as if she had a chill.

"Nonsense," Gram said, stabbing a piece of meat and dropping it onto their mother's plate. "We eat hearty in this household. Because we all work hard." She put a piece on her own plate and smacked her lips. "Venison burgers right off the grill. I don't guess we've done them like this in years, have we, Babe?"

"N-nope. I don't guess in y-years," he echoed, stabbing one and then passing the plate to Carrot.

Carrot looked around the table at Gram, her face red and cheerful above her faded corduroy shirt, and then at her mother, staring silently down at her plate, and at Babe, rocking back and forth like a fat clown, shoveling boiled potatoes into his mouth. And finally at Beaut, taking dainty bites of her burger, wiping the crumbs off her green sweater, as if this were an ordinary dinner.

Carrot remembered a blue water-pitcher they had kept on the table at home. She felt like she was the blue pitcher filled to the brim with tears. She blinked hard at her plate, then put down her burger. "Is this the way it's going to be?" she asked.

Gram reached out and took one of Carrot's hands in her strong brown one. "Carissa Alyssa Turvy, what's wrong with you?"

Wrong? She wanted to get up on Gram's old, rickety chair and scream it. She wanted to stand on the table and kick the plates of food into the air. But she saw her mother's eyes squeeze shut, the quivering of her lip. "I'm not hungry," she said. And she jumped up and ran through the living room, past the moose and out the back door into the spring night.

2

In the morning Carrot woke up to Beaut's voice. For a second she thought they were back home and that Beaut had come in to wake her for school. But then she saw Gram's weathered gray pie-safe that served as the bedroom dresser and Beaut standing beside it in her long nightie. She was pumping her arms and tossing her head like a boxer.

Carrot untangled herself from the quilt. "What are you doing?"

Beaut turned around and looked at Carrot, her hands on her hips. "Are you deaf? That dumb chicken woke me up hours ago. Honestly, I don't know how Gram stands that squawking, day after day. Anyway, watch this and tell me what you think." Beaut reached back to pull two dresser scarves from the top of the pie safe and turned back around to face Carrot. She started the boxing routine again, moving her body from side to side and shaking the dresser scarves like pom-poms: "Up-ward, on-ward, old Pee-lee. Lead us on to vic-tor-y." After she yelled it three

7

times she jumped, throwing the scarves into the air. "Well?" She looked at Carrot.

"It was okay," Carrot said, wondering why Beaut was trying so hard.

"Honest? Did you really like it?"

"Not really," Carrot said, fingering a red-and-black plaid quilt patch, the same as one of Babe's shirts. "I like 'stronger than a hurricane, braver than an eagle, we're the cream, we're the team, we're mighty, fighting Regal.'"

"Yeah," Beaut sighed, sitting on the edge of the bed.

"You were the best cheerleader Regal ever had." Carrot slid over beside her sister, glad that they had to share this bedroom. It was comforting to have Beaut to curl up next to all night long. "Don't worry, you'll make Peelee's team. No sweat."

"I hope you're right," Beaut said. "If I don't, I'll just die." She picked up a hairbrush and began attacking Carrot's wild tangle of hair.

"Don't say that," Carrot said, snatching the hairbrush.

"C'mon, Care." Beaut put her arm around her sister. "We have to act normal Gram said. The more normal you act, the more normal you feel." She squeezed Carrot tighter so she could look over her shoulder at the clock. "You better start by getting ready for school."

Carrot groaned. "I can't go to school, Beaut. I can't. I know I'm behind in math and everything and they probably do everything way different than at Regal."

Beaut sighed. "We shouldn't have stayed out for a whole month. It makes it twice as hard to start now."

"It was Mom's fault," Carrot said. "If it hadn't been for

Gram, she would have kept us out the rest of the year. Mushbrain."

"She's not a mushbrain," Beaut said. "Don't you think she had a lot on her mind? She had the house to sell and besides she was upset." Beaut looked at the clock again. "We have to get moving, Care. Want to use the shower?"

Carrot shook her head and started pulling off her pajamas. "*She* didn't do anything. Gram sold the house. She packed up everything and moved us here." Then she realized that Beaut was already down the hall, running water. "Gram should have left us alone," she said bitterly.

Beaut was as quiet as Carrot when they got on the bus. She led Carrot to the first empty seats and didn't even look around when some boy in the back whistled through his teeth. Boys were always whistling at Beaut. She was as unlike Carrot as a rose from a blade of grass. While Carrot's red hair was stuffed up in a baseball cap, Beaut's hair hung in soft yellow curls over her shoulders, and today she had tied a ribbon around it to match her shirt. Beaut had eyes as green as the fern garden in the middle of Gram's woods and her smile was for everyone she met. Except this morning. She seemed as nervous as Carrot.

When they got off the bus in front of the brown brick box that was both Peelee Junior and Peelee Senior, they stood there watching the kids breeze by, laughing, yelling across the lawns, some of them arm in arm. A couple of younger kids were on skateboards.

"Ding-a-lings," Carrot said.

"Come on, Carrot," said Beaut, frowning. "They're just

like the kids from Regal." She paused. "Well, the boys do wear their hair a little longer. And none of the girls at Regal would wear regular white tennis shoes." She took a deep breath. "What's your first class?"

"English," Carrot said. She pinched a piece of Beaut's pink, flowered shirt between her fingers and held on tightly as Beaut walked her up the three cement steps and into the building.

"It's so tiny," Beaut whispered. "It looks like the Regal Park Play School."

Carrot stared down the dark hallway to her right. It was a maze. Yelling kids bumped down the narrow passage like cattle, dodging locker doors that opened and shut with a hundred clangs. She wanted to cover her ears. "It's jammed," she said to Beaut. "Maybe there won't be any room for us."

Beaut walked her down the hall to room 115. "This is where your English class meets," she said. "I've got to go upstairs. Wait for me at the bus after school."

"Beaut," Carrot pleaded, clinging to her shirt.

"Just act like a normal thirteen year old. And smile," she said, patting Carrot's cheek. Her shirt slid through Carrot's fingers as she disappeared.

Carrot walked into the class and stopped beside a big blond desk. Behind it sat a big blond woman in a red dress who smiled at Carrot.

"You must be Carrie Turvy."

Carrot nodded.

"I'm Mrs. Smoznak, purveyor of good grammar, good literature, and, I hope, good fellowship." She swept a red arm toward the back of the room. "If you see an empty desk along the wall, take it."

Carrot nodded again. Hugging her books she walked quickly down the aisle so it would look like she knew what she was doing. And she slid into the nearest empty desk along the back wall, stuffing her books in the basket under the seat like everyone else did. Instantly her books crashed to the floor. All of her pencils went rolling toward the front of the class.

A girl with bright red-rimmed glasses turned around and giggled. "You got the desk with the broken basket."

Carrot could feel her face getting hot, and she slid down in her seat. The whole class turned around to look at her. Then a boy four rows down leaned over and picked up her pencils. "Pencils," he said, and handed them back to the girl behind him. The next girl did the same so it was like a relay and everyone in the class was laughing when the girl with red glasses said, "Pencils," and handed them to Carrot. "You'd better move over," she said, pointing to the next empty desk.

Carrot took the pencils and slunk into the next seat, wishing she had a dozen books to stack on top of the desk so she wouldn't have to look at all the stupid, grinning faces.

Mrs. Smoznak wrote something on the board: "You must believe to achieve." Then she came around to the front of her desk. "All right, class," she said, "we've got a lot of work to get through today so let's get going. But before we do, are there any world records?"

A fat boy in shiny black pants stood up. "It's my birthday." While everyone cheered and clapped he made a formal bow.

A girl wearing a bunch of colored beads around her neck stood up. "Look." She stuck out her leg.

"Hallelujah," Mrs. Smoznak said, clapping her hands. "I hope you saved your cast with all our signatures on it."

The girl giggled and twisted her fingers in her beads. "My father shellacked it for me and my mom is going to fill it with straw flowers."

Mrs. Smoznak laughed and the whole class cheered. Carrot sank deeper into her seat. What did all this dumb stuff have to do with English?

Mrs. Smoznak rapped on her desk with her knuckles. "Okay, class, I would like you to pass your diagramed sentences forward, and then we're going to read our essays aloud." She half sat on the front of her desk and folded her arms under her large bosom, looking around the room. "Robert," she said, pointing at a boy to Carrot's right, over by the windows, "would you be our first volunteer?"

From the way everyone groaned this was supposed to be a joke. Robert stood up and shuffled his feet a few times, then cleared his throat. "Umm," he said, "it's not quite two hundred and fifty words."

She nodded. "Go ahead."

"My father is a school bus driver. His name is"— he looked up and shrugged—"you know, Mr. Miles. But all the little kids call him Mr. Smiles because he smiles a lot. Except when I leave his wrenches out in the rain. Then he—"

Carrot tried not to listen to Robert's essay. She pictured what she would do back at Gram's. Though they had moved in over a week ago she couldn't think of it as home. Gram's was a place where she never had to think about school and essay writing and acting grown up. Would it still be all right, she wondered, to stack green apples on top of the fence posts and shoot them off? Was Bing, her tin deer, still around, abandoned under some pine tree? Would she ever find him? Would any of it feel the same again?

Somebody else, a girl with stiff, bird's-nest hair, was reading now. "My father," she began, and Carrot felt like somebody had reached into her chest and crumpled her heart into a little ball. These were the stupidest essays she had ever heard. She didn't want to hear about anyone's father. She grabbed a pencil off her desk and began clicking it up and down in her mouth, listening to the sound it made as it hit her teeth. Like the hollow sound of woodpeckers hammering in Gram's woods. Clicking the pencil she looked out the window at the straight dark row of pines at the border of the school grounds. She wondered if deer ever came to the edge of the pines and looked at all this confusion. If they had any sense they would never come out; they would stay curled up in a snug thicket till every kid, every teacher, went home. She turned her head from side to side, pretending she was a deer, still clicking the pencil in her mouth.

When the bird's-nest girl had finished reading Carrot looked back toward the front of the room and saw that Mrs. Smoznak was watching her.

"Class," she said, "I almost forgot to introduce our

newest member, Carrie Turvy. She has just moved here from Regal. That's down near Detroit, isn't it, Carrie?"

Carrot ripped the pencil out of her mouth and nodded.

"Why don't you stand up, Carrie, and tell us a little about yourself, your family, your hobbies?"

Carefully Carrot slid out of her seat, making sure her pencil was secure in the pencil well. She could feel the whole class shift in their seats so they could look at her. The girl with the red-rimmed glasses was smiling up at her like Carrot was going to tell them some big, fat fairy tale.

"I—well, I have a sister and a—a, well, I like to—" She almost said "hunt," but that wasn't right. "I like to walk in the woods on my grandmother's farm and, umm, that's about it," she said stupidly. She started to sit down.

"Since you have to listen to all our Dad essays, why don't you tell us a few things about your father? Just tell us what he likes to do, maybe what he looks like. Does he sing in the shower?" She lifted both hands in the air. "Anything at all."

Carrot's heart started pounding furiously. What could she say? She looked at Mrs. Smoznak helplessly. "My—" She swallowed and felt the burning in her eyelids. Twenty-three jerky-looking kids were turned to listen to her say something wonderful about her father. Her father that they had left in Regal under six feet of dirt and a blanket of red roses. She closed her eyes and tried to make the faces disappear. But when she opened them they were all staring at her. "No," she whispered. Then, louder, "No."

She was running up the aisle, bumping desks and scattering books as she came. Through her tears she had a glimpse of Mrs. Smoznak coming for her, hands out.

"Nooo," she yelled again, flinging her arm out. She was

running, running down the narrow hall, her tennis shoes going *pockity, pockity,* her jacket flying out behind her. Where was the door? Where was the door? A teacher stuck his head out and yelled, "Hey—slow down!" But she kept running till she came to a door with sunlit windows and she heaved herself against it and the door fell open and she was outside in the sunshine. She heard baby birds chirping high up on the building but she didn't look up, she didn't look back.

She turned right from the school yard and ran down Washton toward Bentley. Bentley, she knew, would take her to Gram's. She ran on past a hardware store with a big American flag in the window, and a gray building— "Showbiz Family Video"—where a lady was just coming out, pushing a baby in a stroller. She saw the lady stop and stare at her like she was crazy, so Carrot pulled up the collar of her big jacket to hide her face and kept running, wondering if the lady would report her to the police. She ran past all the shops and then past Our Lady of Refuge Catholic Church, where bells rang overhead. The sound followed her down the street past a long stretch of little houses—yellow, green, and pink, like mints at a birthday party. Or at a funeral, she thought. And then she couldn't stop it any longer.

She was back at the house in Regal, straddling the kitchen chair backward, having the same old argument with her mother.

"I don't want to go to your dumb old makeup show and pass out cookies and wear some cheesy dress. This is our weekend for Gram's."

"The decision is made. I already discussed it with your

15

father," her mother said in the shrill voice she used when she knew Carrot was going to give her an argument.

"Yeah, and he said I could make up my own mind."

"You cannot make up your own mind. I'm beginning to wonder if you have a mind. Thirteen and a half years old, and still running around in the woods like a—a chipmunk." She pressed her hand to her forehead and sighed loudly. "Honestly, I don't know why I let him start this business with you—going off every other weekend like a couple of savages, shooting up all of northern Michigan. And when you are home you haven't the slightest regard for what I want for you." She sighed again, lifting the hair off her neck like she was posing for a snapshot. "Is it asking too much for you to just be at this show, looking nice, wearing the colors I picked out just for you? Wearing a little smidgen of makeup. Making people look good is my business. What will people think if I can't even make my own daughter look good?" She dropped her hair and took a step toward Carrot. "Darling, you're the perfect autumn. In that purple dress with your hair and your pale skin—"

"No!" Carrot jumped up so violently that she knocked over the chair. "Stop calling me an autumn. I'm not an autumn. I'm not a spring. I'm not a winter. I hate that stuff. I'm just me."

Her mother went stiff as a post and crossed her arms. "I didn't raise you to be a savage, Carrie. And I'm not going to let your father turn you into one. We'll continue this when he gets home."

Carrot stomped out the back door with her mother shrieking behind her, "Come back here and pick up this chair. Come back here. Wait until your father gets home."

She should have picked up the chair and put it back where it belonged. Then her mother wouldn't have had to say that last thing about her father. Then maybe he would have come home just like always, in his saggy jeans and dark blue Work Force Building Company T-shirt. He would have popped a beer and stuck his finger in whatever pot was cooking on the stove. And then he would have said, "Susan, Carrot would be the worst model in the world for you. She would look like a monkey that somebody tried to dress up like a prom queen. Just use Beaut again; she's your prom queen material."

But what if he had said to her, "Just put the purple dress on and go to the silly shindig, Carrot. Prove to your mother that you're not a savage." She would have done it! She would have gone to a thousand of her mother's makeup shows if only she could take back what happened. Now she couldn't change anything. It kept running behind her eyelids like in a movie. Her father, falling from the peak of somebody's gray-shingled roof, his hammer still upraised in his hand, like the man in the Sparky's Hardware ad. It wasn't so far, that fall, not far enough to kill a person. It was his heart they said; it wasn't the little fall through the blue spring sky. But how it hurt to feel him hit the ground.

Now her arms came up to catch him, until she realized how stupid she looked running with her arms up in the air. She stopped at the top of the hill leading down to Gram's driveway. Catching the sleeve of the big canvas jacket in her hand she wiped her nose. She pushed back the snarl of red hair. Somewhere she had lost the baseball cap. Her face was sticky with dried tears but she couldn't go into Gram's to wash off. She was home five hours too early.

Besides, with her mother there, Gram's had lost its magic. But outside there was no one to remind her she was a little savage. Walking around in Gram's woods and fields she could be the person she wanted to be. If she couldn't share that person with her father anymore there was nobody in the world she could share it with. She took a deep breath and started down the hill.

3

*C*arrot sat on a stump watching a red squirrel. It was jumping in a circle around the base of an oak, bouncing up and down like a rubber ball. Carrot had pulled an old piece of toast from Gram's compost pile and was about to toss it to the squirrel when, from the corner of her eye, she saw Beaut's shirt and shorts moving up the long drive. Carrot put her fingers to her mouth and whistled.

Beaut stopped and looked around, her hair shimmering like a halo in the sunlight.

"Beaut!" Carrot started running down the slope, along the cornfield, not stopping even when Beaut saw her. Running always felt better to her than walking—it was like putting distance between herself and her troubles. But now, seeing Beaut, hugging her books to her chest, reminded Carrot that besides being a jerk in Mrs. Smoznak's class she had left all her books behind.

"Carrie Turvy, where were you? I waited and waited. I even made the bus driver wait while I ran back to your locker and looked for you." She tossed her hair and glared at Carrot.

"I—I missed the bus," Carrot said feebly.

"I *know* you missed the bus, Care. *Why* did you miss the bus?"

"Well—I—listen, don't tell Mom, okay?" Her mother wouldn't have cared about the missed classes but she'd go into orbit if she found out about the big scene in English. "I just—I forgot my books and I walked home."

Beaut rolled her eyes and looked at the sky. "You walked all the way home? Five miles? Why didn't you just call Gram? Are you crazy? And anyway, how did you beat me home?"

Before Carrot could say anything, Babe came out of the chicken shed, waving his arms. "Carrot—Beaut—the chicks are pipping. Henny Penny has ten already. Little teensy baby chicks. I counted ten of them, peeping and peeping. And they're fuzzing up. Come and see. Carrot, you can pick them up if you're careful. C'mon, Beaut—you too. Come and see."

Babe took Carrot's hand and started tugging her toward the chicken coop, which leaned toward the south side of the house like a squashed red shoebox.

"Oh, Babe," Beaut said, shaking her head. "I have to go in and change so I can practice for cheerleading tryouts. I only have ten more days. Carrot, you go." Beaut waved them off.

"Don't you say anything," Carrot yelled hotly over her shoulder as Beaut pranced away up the drive.

Babe was pulling with both hands. "C'mon, Carrot—you

never seen anything like them. You never been here when they first brooded."

"Hang on, Babe." Carrot pulled away and put her hand over her eyes. She had spent all afternoon walking around in the woods, smelling the sweetness of new lilacs, watching a pair of orioles building a nest, walking and walking, trying to forget what happened in English class, trying to forget everything. She wasn't ready to let go of that stillness, even for Babe. She felt like one of the little china shoes in her mother's collection. Breakable. Carrot took her hand away and looked at Babe's wide-eyed smile above the red bow tie. He got so excited, more like a seven-year-old boy than a thirty-five-year-old man. And she knew he would never take no for an answer. He'd bug her until she gave in. Her father always said Babe would have made a great politician if he weren't so honest.

Carrot put her finger to Babe's lips. "Whisper," she whispered.

"Are your nerves a-atwitter?" Babe whispered, his eyes opening wider.

Carrot laughed. Atwitter nerves was what her mother always had. "Forget it," she said, taking his hand again.

Once inside the chicken coop she forgot about feeling breakable. "Oooh," she squealed, kneeling beside Babe on the straw-covered floor. "Look at Henny Penny—she's gigantic."

Henny Penny squatted, enormous and red, inside a big wooden crate. Her feathers were all puffed out to cover the chicks who were peeping frantically underneath her. Babe and Carrot watched as two little orange chicks pushed out from under a wing and stumbled forward.

"They're so tiny," Carrot whispered.

Babe bent over and scooped up one of the orange balls and held it out to her. As soon as Carrot took it Henny Penny began clucking wildly. She jabbed her head forward and shrieked at Carrot as if her throat would split.

"Shhhh, shhhh." Babe stroked Henny Penny's back. "Carrot will be careful, Henny Penny. You'll see, Carrot won't hurt your baby. Say it, Carrot, say it," he urged.

"Oh, no," Carrot breathed. "I'll be very gentle. Very, very gentle," she whispered. The chick sat calmly in her hand, his bright black eyes studying her. She could feel his steady breathing, in and out, in and out, and the delicate bones of his little body. Watching, to make sure Henny Penny didn't object, she brought the chick up to her face and brushed the soft down against her cheek. The tight ball of pain inside her began to loosen. "It's so soft," she whispered.

"S-soft as a cloud," Babe said. He picked up another chick and held it against his fat pink cheek. "Peep, peep, peep, peep," he said. He and Carrot laughed when the chick peeped right along with him. "I love you little Ch-Chicken Little. Pretty soon you're going to be Chicken Big." He lifted the chick in his hand and stroked the top of its head with his thick finger. "I got to get some feed," he said, only half rising so his head wouldn't hit the low, slanted ceiling. "You can stay and play with them while I get the bucket and collect the eggs. Don't move, Carrot. Just stay there and hold the chicks and then you'll feel better."

Carrot smiled up at Babe. He could always tell when she

was in a lousy mood. When she was the most prickly Babe was the most gentle. When she felt like committing murder Babe was the most forgiving. His big, laughing face was so much like her father's that she had to look away. Babe's gestures, the way he scratched the top of his head, or propped his toast on his knuckle and thumb when he ate, or threw back his head in laughter, brought her father back a hundred ways. Like her father Babe loved the whole outdoors—the woods, the fields, the streams.

Now he bent over and with both hands settled the little chick onto the straw like it was a ball of dandelion fluff, and they watched it dart back under the mahogany red coverlet of Henny Penny's body. She clucked scoldingly until the chick was settled and then she settled herself. Satisfied, Babe lumbered over to behind the partition where the hens were. Pretty soon Carrot could hear him talking to the hens, clucking and laughing, praising them for their eggs, shooing them out of his way.

She set the little chick down inside its box and watched him stumble forward until he ran into the wall. Henny Penny clucked and he righted himself and darted forward under her wing and disappeared. She thought how helpless the chicks were and yet how, pretty soon, they would be out scratching for bugs in the yard just like the hens. They didn't need school to teach them how to grow up or how to lay eggs. They didn't have to fuss with makeup or fancy clothes. They just had to be. She took a deep breath, inhaling the sharp, warm odor of ammonia, the musty smell of straw and feathers. It was comforting in the hen house. Simple and comforting.

In a few minutes Babe came back around the partition

with a basket of brown eggs. "Hey, Carrot, you wanna see my eggs? I gotta delivery tomorrow. Mr. Eggs delivers on Tuesday, Thursday, and Saturday. See—twenty—I think twenty. One, two, three—" He continued to move his lips, counting softly, while Carrot watched the chicks take turns popping out from Henny Penny's protection and then darting back under when she clucked. She watched Babe pour a stream of gravelly looking feed into a red cylinder that fed into a red plastic trough. He checked the upturned water jar and lifted one of the little chicks out of the metal pan. "Outa there," he scolded, shaking his finger at the chick. "This is to drink not to fool around in. You wanna grow up to be a fat Henny Penny, don't you? Who's gonna give us eggs if you don't eat and drink like you're supposta?" Henny Penny started squawking and Babe put the chick back down.

Carrot followed him out of the coop, waiting while he carefully locked the chicken-wire gate and moved the cinder block up against it to hold it tight. "C'mon, Carrot," he said, taking her hand again. "We gotta eat, too."

With Babe's big hand around hers, Carrot felt better. Her heart no longer felt ready to shatter into a million pieces. Her stomach growled. She hadn't eaten since breakfast. "Peep, peep, peep," she said.

Babe turned and looked at her, his jaw hanging. Then his lips spread in a slow grin. "Peep, peep, peep," he said, hunching his shoulders in delight.

At dinner Gram sat at the corner, opposite Babe, with Beaut on the end and Carrot on the other side of Gram and her mother next to Babe. Just like the night before,

Carrot thought, wondering why things were exactly one way for years and years and then suddenly you had to do things exactly another way.

"How was school today, my lassies?" Gram asked between bites of chicken stew. "Did you march in there like proud Turvys and show them what we're made of?" As soon as she asked the question the telephone rang. "Oh, bother," she grumbled, putting down her fork. "It doesn't ring all day and then when you try to sit down and eat— there it goes."

"I got new chicks." Babe looked at Mom who was wearing the same pale robe from the night before. "They just pipped."

She lifted her eyes from her plate and shuddered. "Pipped?" she said. "Oh, Babe. Not at the dinner table."

"Ten of 'em," he said, wiping his milk mustache with the back of his hand and then holding up all ten fingers. "The others are gonna pip tonight, maybe. You wanna see 'em?"

Ignoring Babe, Mom reached over and tucked a frizzy hank of Carrot's hair behind her ears. "If you would at least let me French-braid it."

Carrot sighed and shook her head so the wayward lock fell forward again. Most animals, except for kittens, either scared or grossed out her mother, so she figured chickens were in the gross-out category. She felt sorry for Babe, and so she said to Beaut, "The little chicks are so cute. They're about this big." She picked the biscuit off her plate and held it up to show her.

Babe giggled and picked up another biscuit and then another to show Beaut until his hands were full of powdery biscuits. "You know," Babe said, rocking back and forth with the biscuits, "these are all going to lay eggs in five months."

"All those eggs," Beaut said, "you're going to be rich, Babe. The Mr. Eggs's Empire."

"Mr. Eggs's Empire," Babe said, blinking at the biscuits. "Thirty dozen—no, I mean forty dozen eggs. That's—" He stopped rocking and looked at Beaut. "How much is that?"

"That's forty dollars, Babe. And now you're going to have ten more layers. You'll have to sell more eggs."

"Yeah," he said dreamily. "I'm gonna buy a television."

Suddenly Gram returned from the other room. "Babe, put those biscuits back in the bowl and stop acting so foolish." She yanked out her chair and sat down, snatching up her napkin and shaking it out with a snap. Instead of picking up her fork she looked at her daughter-in-law. "Susan, that was your daughter's teacher—Carrot's teacher," she said carefully.

Carrot's heart did a flip-flop. She knew what was coming. Her mother would be furious. "Mom, I—"

Gram held up her hand. "This is between your mother and me. This teacher," she went on, "this Mrs. Smoznak says she asked Carrie to get up and say a few words about her father."

Her mother's eyes got big and she put her hand to her mouth.

"The poor thing left the class in tears."

Carrot slumped down in her seat. Gram was going to bring it all back, the class staring at her, running from the classroom, Mrs. Smoznak trying to stop her. She watched her mother's face go white, and then she looked away.

"Didn't you tell them, Susan? Didn't you tell them at the school about Jesse?"

Her mother shook her head. "How could I? How could I say it to a perfect stranger? It's nobody's business about— about any of us."

"Well," Gram folded her hands over her plate, "it *is* somebody's business, Susan. Do you think this teacher ever would have mortified our Carrot in front of the whole class if she had known that her father had just died? Don't you think that's being unfair to Carrot and to the teacher and to Beaut, too, for that matter?"

"Well, I just couldn't," her mother said in a watery voice. "You wouldn't know how much it hurts me, Clara. It just hurts too much."

Gram slapped her napkin to the table. "We all hurt, Susan," she said tartly. "But there's no sense being a jackass about it, just for the satisfaction of keeping your miseries all to yourself. You'd better get a grip on yourself, girl. You have two daughters to raise and we have five mouths to feed here and not much income to speak of. You can't go around like a whimpering fool much longer."

Susan rose, clutching the neck of her bathrobe with both hands. As she watched her mother run up the stairs, Carrot squeezed her biscuit into a powder of dry crumbs.

4

*C*arrot would never love anyone like she loved her
father. That was her first thought when the rooster
crowed the next morning. Ever since she could remember,
from the time she was four or three or maybe younger, she
had followed him around, imitating his bouncing walk,
clomping around in his boots, sitting for hours in his big lap
listening to geese honking or watching the trees shake with
autumn color. "Alder," he would say, picking up the bright
orange leaf and twirling it under her nose. "Maple, cotton-
wood." He would point at the trees as they walked, her
hand lost in his huge one.

And when she was older he took her hunting. Those
November days, away from school, from her mother, her
friends—nothing else mattered. Curled up in the deer
blind with the heater, eating Gram's sandwiches, drinking
from a thermos of sweet, hot coffee, they would spend
hours in silence. He would nod his head to show her a
woodpecker or make a hand sandwich with her when her
fingers got cold. And Babe, too, when he came, learned to

shut up and watch. The times her father shot a deer she would shut her eyes, her teeth chattering in fear, and cling to Babe, too scared to see what had happened to the bright-eyed deer that had bounded through the woods only moments before. That awful part was the price she had to pay for everything else. When it happened she always ran ahead to Gram's, trying not to think about what Babe and her father were dragging through the trees, thinking instead about the celebration, about Gram clanging the big iron triangle by the front door until the whole woods rang. Those weekends on the farm were the best—with Dad and Babe and Gram and Carrot all sitting in front of the fire, under the moose head, eating Gram's blueberry pie. Carrot loved living that way—burning their own firewood, target shooting in the woods, eating Mr. Eggs's omelets for breakfast. Simple. Her father taught her to love the simple things.

The rooster crowed again and Carrot had a second thought. She would never forgive her mother. Her mother had ruined everything for Carrot. And she had ruined everything for her father.

In the bed beside her Beaut groaned and put the pillow over her head.

"Stupid chickens," she muttered.

"It's not the chickens. It's Jupiter, the rooster," Carrot said, glad to be distracted by Beaut's grumpiness.

On the way out to the bus stop Beaut stopped in the driveway. "Look at that squirrel."

Carrot looked where Beaut was pointing beside the chicken coop, and there was the little red squirrel that she had been watching yesterday. It was still hopping up and down as if there were springs in its feet. Watching it gave Carrot a weird feeling. "Something's wrong. It doesn't even stop to rest."

"Maybe it's drunk," Beaut said, giggling.

By the time they got to school Carrot had forgotten the squirrel. She was thinking about going back into her English class. The dark, crowded hallway seemed even more dungeony than yesterday. But Beaut was grinning and waving like a queen on a homecoming float.

"Hey, Arbuta," a girl in a denim shirt called out. "Did you finish the last problem in algebra? Did it give you a nosebleed or what?"

"Oh, hi, Jenny. It was the worst," Beaut called back. Just as if they'd been friends for years.

"Hi, Arbuta," a tall dark-haired boy said.

Beaut smiled as they passed in the hall.

"See you in history," the boy called after her; and Carrot looked over her shoulder to see the boy walking down the hall backward staring at Beaut.

"I hate *Arbuta*," she said to Carrot. "I'm going to tell everyone to call me Beaut, starting today."

Carrot stared at her. "Even the teachers?"

"Well, of course. If the teachers keep calling me Arbuta, everyone else will too."

Carrot squeezed closer to Beaut, wishing some of her courage would rub off. This was only her second day of school and already Beaut had friends, already she was going to talk to her teachers. Carrot wouldn't go up and talk to one of her teachers for a zillion dollars. Even if she was going to throw up in class she wouldn't go up and say anything.

Just ahead was room 115. "I don't want to go in there," she whispered to Beaut. "Everyone will stare at me. Oh, Beaut, can't I go back home?" She stopped in the hall and seized Beaut's hand.

"It will only be hard this once," Beaut said, pushing her forward. "Just go in there and act like you're the most popular girl in the class. And smile." She peeled her hand out of Carrot's and propelled her to the doorway. "See you later," she said, and disappeared.

Carrot took a deep breath, pulled down the visor of Babe's John Deere cap, and stalked into the room. Her face was on fire and she could feel every eye staring at her. She was about to slide into the back row seat when Mrs. Smoznak called her.

"Carrie? Would you come up here?"

Carrot's heart thudded to a stop. She took a deep breath and walked back up the aisle, watching her tennis shoes.

"Let's go out in the hall," Mrs. Smoznak said in a quiet voice, and Carrot couldn't tell if she was really mad or just a little irritated. She watched Mrs. Smoznak's legs move away from her desk, watched the orange border of her dress swish toward the door. She followed, concentrating on a run in the back of Mrs. Smoznak's nylon stocking that went down her leg and into her shoe.

In the hall Mrs. Smoznak said, "You left these yesterday," and handed her books to her. Then, very softly, she said, "Carrie, I'm so sorry. I didn't know about your father."

Carrot's heart felt squeezed again. The burning started in her eyelids. She made her hands into two tight fists and looked away. She stared at the poster across the hall that said PEELEE CHEERLEADING TRYOUTS. Underneath the lettering was a photo of twelve girls in blue sweaters with red *P*'s on them. She would not cry. She would not run. She would think about Beaut doing handsprings and scissors kicks.

"I know this will be a difficult year for you," Mrs. Smoznak went on, "losing your father, moving to a new town, a new school. I want to make it as easy for you as I can and I promise you we all feel that way at Peelee. Your grandmother told me you've missed a month of school. If you can stop by during your study hall, I'll go over some of the things we've been working on—sentence diagraming, personal essays, American poets." When Carrot didn't respond, Mrs. Smoznak said, "Carrot—"

Surprised, Carrot looked up and Mrs. Smoznak smiled her wide, red smile. "Your grandmother calls you Carrot, doesn't she? Your hair is such a pretty color you should take off your cap so we can see the rest of it. Carrot," she said again, and she reached out and put her hands on Carrot's shoulders, "there's one more thing. I'd like to tell the class about your father."

Carrot's mouth flew open.

"People want to help, Carrot. And they can if you let them."

Carrot thought about all the kids in English class talking about her father's accident, about his death, about Carrot running out of class in tears because her father was dead. What did that mean to them—"her father"? It meant that she was someone to stare at, someone to whisper about. Carrot didn't need to be a big show; she needed to be invisible. For once her mother was right. This was not something to be shared with strangers. It was something very private. "No," she said. "I don't need anything."

Mrs. Smoznak smiled. "I think you're wrong, Carrot. We all need each other. But the decision is up to you."

She didn't say anything more for a moment and neither did Carrot. Mrs. Smoznak's perfume hung in the air between them, reminding Carrot of the fragrance of the snowball bush beside Gram's house. "No," she said again.

"Okay," Mrs. Smoznak said. She gave Carrot's shoulders a squeeze and led her back into the room.

The rest of the day Carrot hurried to her classes so she would arrive before anyone else, and she left as soon as the bell rang so she wouldn't have to talk to anyone. In math a girl with braces tapped her on the shoulder. When Carrot turned around, she asked, "Are you new?"

Carrot nodded, and turned back and stuck her head in her math book like she was fascinated by fractions. The girl didn't bother her again.

At the end of the day Carrot stood off by herself against the side of the school building, waiting for Beaut. She stood under a maple tree away from the buses and watched the kids come out of the building. They were laughing and yelling and chasing each other. One boy took a girl's tennis shoe and threw it to another boy while the girl ran in one stocking foot after first one boy and then the other. Another boy was piggybacking a girl who was bigger than he was, and her rear hung down almost to the sidewalk. In a minute Carrot spotted Beaut coming out the door in her purple miniskirt. She was walking with two girls and the tall boy who had said hi to her in the hall. Carrot hung back, waiting for Beaut to look in her direction, but she walked to bus number seven with the others and didn't turn around till she started up the bus steps. When she spotted Carrot huddled under the tree she said something to one of the girls and waved her arm to Carrot. Then they both got on the bus.

When Carrot got there Beaut was sitting with the other girl.

Carrot stood in the aisle and glared at Beaut.

"Oh, hi, Carrot," Beaut said, finally looking up. "This is Nicole."

Carrot didn't say anything when Nicole said hi. She just stood there in the aisle, clutching her books while kids bumped past her down the aisle. If Beaut wasn't going to sit with her she wouldn't sit with anyone else. She would stand up in the aisle for the entire ride.

Finally Beaut sighed, "Nicole, I'm going to go back and sit with my sister. I'll see you tomorrow, okay?" She got up and nudged Carrot toward the back of the bus. When they sat down Beaut hissed, "Carrot, for god's sake, what's wrong with you?"

"You have to sit with me. You promised," Carrot muttered.

"I didn't think it was such a big deal," Beaut said, stonily. "I thought maybe you'd have met a friend to sit with. I thought maybe I could spend a few minutes talking to Nicole, who just happens to be a cheerleader and who was going to give me some pointers. I just thought maybe I could have a little fun for a change without being reminded of—" She stopped and dropped her chin into her hand and looked out the window.

They were passing a green farm—the house, the silo, and two barns were all the color of new leaves. The farm was surrounded by a white fence, with cows hanging their brown and white faces over it, chewing soberly. Some boys ahead of them pressed up against the bus window and went, "Moo-oo-oo." They did it morning and after-noon, every time they passed the cows. Then they started giggling and snorting, punching each other and throwing pencils in the air until the bus driver yelled at them.

Carrot huddled closer to Beaut, wishing she weren't so angry. When they got off the bus Beaut started down the long drive without her. Carrot jogged to catch up. "Why are you so mad?"

Beaut answered without looking at Carrot, "I keep telling myself, try to act normal, try to act normal. And I try to smile at everyone and talk to everyone and dress nice and not think about—not think about what happened. And, Carrot"—she stopped and looked at Carrot, her eyes shimmering with tears—"all you do is make things worse. You complain and fight with Mom and say how terrible everything is and—and I hate that—that—" She shook her head and started walking again.

"You hate what?" Carrot asked, jogging again.

"I hate that jacket," Beaut said, staring straight ahead. "Do you have to wear it every single solitary day of your life? You look like a war orphan or something."

Carrot felt the worn canvas brushing against her arms as she ran, felt the softness against her knuckles balled up in the deep pockets. Her father had worn the dun-colored jacket for as long as she could remember, filling the pockets with screwdrivers, cartridges, extra socks, binoculars, candy, and blue balloons for target practice. From the time she was five she had nestled against the jacket as she and her father sat in his deer blind or sometimes under an umbrella of colored leaves, listening to the rustling of the trees, the chatter of birds, the light, nervous bounding and stopping of deer off in the woods. It didn't matter to Carrot if she looked like a war orphan. She would wear her father's jacket until she was an old lady like Gram. It was like having his arms around her. But she didn't say this to Beaut. She just jogged beside her like a puppy, trying to keep up.

Beaut stopped again. "Look."

It was the squirrel, still hopping beside the chicken coop. In the May sunshine the bouncing squirrel looked like a windup toy left in the grass by a child. "It must be sick," Carrot said. "I'd better tell Gram."

They found Gram in the kitchen, scouring the inside of an old pickle crock. She looked up, red-faced; a tumble of gray hair had frizzed out from her braid. "Oh, bother, is it that late already? I was going to do up some rolls and I haven't even got out the cartons for Mr. Eggs. And your mother was supposed to—" She looked at Carrot's face. "What's wrong?"

"There's a squirrel outside and he's acting real funny. He's been bouncing up and down since yesterday."

Gram and Beaut and Carrot went out the back door past the Chinese elm to the back of the shed. Even before they saw the squirrel they saw his shadow, bouncing on the grass.

"Poor little mite," Gram said, shaking her head. "He's

got something pretty bad. Could be he fell out of a nest on his head, but it could be a sickness."

Just then Babe came out from the other side of the chicken shed with a basket of eggs. He broke into a grin when he saw Beaut and Carrot.

"Get over here, Babe," Gram called sharply.

Babe stood next to Carrot and looked at the squirrel. It stopped for a moment and lay limp in the grass like an old chamois cloth. In another moment it started bouncing again. Sighing heavily, Babe watched it. He set his basket of eggs down and began to wring his big hands. "Couldn't I go get it, Mama, and bring it to the house?"

Gram put her hand out in front of Babe like a crossing guard. "You stay right where you are, mister. That squirrel might just take a bite out of you that could put you in a bad way." She shook her head. "This poor fella is going to die and the sooner the better."

Babe looked at Carrot. "You see, Carrot, he can't stop jumping. He wishes he could but he can't."

Carrot nodded, feeling sick inside. She thought of the squirrel jumping and jumping all day and all night and all day, not able to eat or sleep or run away from other animals. It had a strange electricity running through its body that changed it from a squirrel running around gathering nuts and skittering up trees to some weird machine that didn't know what it was. Like Gram, she knew the best thing for it was to die quickly. She looked at her grandmother who put her arm around her shoulder.

"Do you want to put it down?" Gram asked.

Carrot's heart suddenly leaped in her chest. In all the years of hunting with her father she had never shot a thing.

She could shoot Bing, her tin deer, dead center in the heart, she could shoot an apple off a fence post at a hundred yards, but she couldn't pull the trigger on a living thing, not on a deer, not even on a pheasant.

"Couldn't we just let it die?" She looked again at her grandmother, her eyes pleading with her not to make her do it.

Gram nodded. "We could."

The four of them stood there silently, watching the squirrel leaping and twisting in the air like a circus performer. Carrot began to feel the squirrel's terror, surrounded by four giants and helpless to run away. So small and so exhausted. How long could it go on? She knew it could be days before it thrashed itself to death. Watching it fling itself skyward over and over she felt embarrassed at her hesitation. She let out a long breath. "I'll do it, Gram."

"I can't watch," Beaut said, and went inside when Carrot went back for her rifle. Carrot walked back and raised the gun. She watched the squirrel jump and land a final time. Her shot rang out over Gram's sunlit acreage, stopping all bird-chittering, wind-rustling, chick-peeping sounds and leaving a vast, ringing silence.

Carrot walked over to the dead squirrel and looked at its small, broken body, the wound bleeding bright copper in the sunlight. She closed her eyes and breathed in, imagining herself far away in the deep woods, beyond this moment, curled into a sweet silence, where death on this May afternoon wasn't even a possibility. She imagined the brush of maple saplings against her skin, the musky smell of bogs.

"Is he dead?" Babe nudged her. "Carrot?"

She knelt down to touch the beautiful red tail. "I'm sorry," she whispered.

Gram put her arm around Carrot as they walked to the house. And Babe patted the top of her head. "Thank you, Carrot. That's what Mr. Squirrel says. Thank you."

Carrot looked up at him and tried to smile. Then she saw her mother standing in the doorway, staring at Carrot with a stricken look on her face.

5

The squirrel started it all over again.

"How could you, Carissa?" her mother asked, white-faced and trembling. "Shooting a poor, defenseless baby squirrel. It's unforgivable, it's—"

"It was a sick squirrel, Susan," Gram said sharply. "It was a kindness Carrot did."

"Sick!" Her mother turned on Gram. "*I'm* sick. She might as well have taken that rifle and shot me right through the heart. I cannot bear a child of mine going around shooting things. It's dreadful, it's shameful, it's unseemly."

"She is *not* dreadful, shameful, or unseemly," Gram said, drawing herself up to her full height, "and neither was her father, who, if you'll recollect, went around shooting a lot more things than Carrot ever did."

"She's a girl." Her mother jabbed the air with her finger. "Girls don't do those things. Killing animals for the fun of it. That's what men do. That's what her father did."

"No!" Gram and Carrot both said it at the same time.

"It was food," Carrot said in a shaky voice. "It was always for food."

"I never heard tell of you turning your nose up at venison steak or rabbit stew," Gram said. "And I don't know how Babe and I would have gotten by without Jess filling our freezer every winter. There's nothing wrong with feeding your family." Gram sniffed and marched off down the hall.

Carrot looked at her mother. "It was going to die, Mom."

Her mother closed her eyes and shook her head, not speaking for a moment. "Why didn't I stop this at the very instant? Ten years ago when she insisted on following him everywhere—into the woods, into the deer blind, like some kind of silly puppy. I have a daughter who goes around killing things. I can't believe it," she whispered.

"I don't," Carrot said stubbornly. "I don't go around killing things."

"Beaut doesn't kill things. She's cheerful. She makes friends. She works hard and puts on her best face every day."

"Carrot isn't me, Mom," Beaut said. "We don't like the same things. We don't dress the same way. That doesn't mean she's a freak."

"Maybe I am a freak," Carrot whispered to Beaut on the way to school the next morning. "I don't look like anyone on this bus."

Beaut studied Carrot. "Mom's right, you know. Your hair is your best feature. Why hide it under that ugly cap? And, Carrot, that T-shirt is four years old. I tie-dyed it in

41

Girl Scouts when I was twelve. But that jacket is the worst. *That* has got to go."

"No." Carrot seized the corduroy lapels as if Beaut was going to snatch it off her body. She shook her head. "I know I'm not bright and friendly like you are. I hate school and I don't want to be a cheerleader and I don't have any friends. And I have a crummy attitude. I'm a freak with a crummy attitude."

"That's not what I meant," said Beaut. "Just because you're not some kind of academic genius and just because you don't want to jump up and down for the football team and just because you killed that squirrel does not make you a freak."

"You killed a squirrel? You? Little Carrot?"

It was Nicole, leaning over the bus seat with a grin on her face.

Carrot slumped down and looked out the window.

"Oh, hi, Nicole," Beaut said, twisting around in her seat. "I tried to call you last night to find out if the tower has five cheerleaders or seven."

"Seven," Nicole said. "But they won't ask us to do that at tryouts. Just individual stuff. So, Carrot, why'd you kill the squirrel?"

Carrot continued to stare out the window, so Beaut answered. "There was a sick squirrel in our yard and Gram asked Carrot to shoot it."

"Wow," Nicole said. "She hunts," she said to the girl next to her. "With a gun and everything."

Carrot shrugged. She didn't know if Nicole was impressed or was just making fun of her. Pretty soon Beaut and Nicole and the other girl were talking about cheer-

42

leading, and the boys in the middle of the bus started mooing, and Carrot put the squirrel out of her mind.

When she walked into English Carrot scooted past Mrs. Smoznak so she wouldn't ask Carrot why she hadn't come for help during her study hall. As usual, Mrs. Smoznak was writing something on the board. Carrot read it from her seat, wondering why she wrote such goofy things every day: "What you are is perfect imperfection." When the bell rang Mrs. Smoznak came in front of her desk with a thick book in her hand. "You know, kids, I think we're going to finish this before school is out. Can you believe it? Only sixty-one pages to go." She thumbed through the book, finding her page, but then she put it down. "Golly," she said, shaking her head. "Our friend Carrot is going to be lost."

There was a ripple of laughter. "Carrot?" someone said.

Mrs. Smoznak looked at Carrot. "Have you read *Moby-Dick*?"

Carrot shook her head, wishing she wasn't the center of attention again.

"Well, class," Mrs. Smoznak asked, "do you think we can tell her the story so far?" Without waiting for a reply, she added, "Robert, would you be our first volunteer?"

Robert groaned. "But you volunteered me first on Monday."

Mrs. Smoznak merely smiled and waved her hand at him to proceed, so Robert turned in his seat to face Carrot. "There was this guy named Ishmael," he said, "who got bored being a schoolteacher—"

Everyone started to laugh.

Mrs. Smoznak crossed her hands over her chest and said,

"In a million years, you kids could never bore me. Drive me crazy, yes. Wear me out, yes. But never bore me."

Robert continued, "So he hooks up with this cannibal guy named Queequeg who he's afraid is going to eat him. But after Queequeg gives him a shrunken head Ishmael sees that he is really a neat guy and they become friends and they both sign up to be harpooners on a whaleboat."

"And the name of the whaleboat?" Mrs. Smoznak asked.

"*The Pequod*," said a heavy girl with spiked brown hair.

"Okay, Brenda. Why don't you continue?"

Now Brenda turned around in her seat and started talking to Carrot. "So okay. The captain is Ahab and he's this really wild character who's got this—like this obsession with a big fat whale named Moby-Dick. And Moby-Dick's the reason he's got this wooden leg. Oh, did I tell you he's got this wooden leg?"

Carrot shook her head.

"Wooden leg?" Mrs. Smoznak repeated.

"Oops!" Brenda said, clapping her hand over her mouth. "It's a whalebone leg because Moby-Dick ate Ahab's real leg. So anyway, Captain Ahab offers a gold piece to whoever spots Moby-Dick, and every time they meet another whaling boat Ahab says, 'Ahoy, did you see Moby-Dick?' Everyone like warns him not to chase Moby but Ahab won't listen to reason. He's got this—you know—this obsession."

"Thank you, Brenda." Mrs. Smoznak pointed at a tall boy with black hair, and ears that stuck out. "Dan."

Dan turned in his seat and stretched his long legs out in the aisle. "So, Carrot," he said, putting his hands behind his head, "in between looking for Moby-Dick, *The Pequod* chased these other whales and Queequeg harpooned a biggie that they had to lash to the boat. And Ishmael and Queequeg and all the rest of them had to climb out on the whale and cut off all its blubber. And the sharks were snapping all around, eating hunks of whale meat and it was a pretty scary job. It wasn't like working at the Dairy Delite, I'll tell you."

"What did they use the blubber for?" Mrs. Smoznak asked.

"Blubber sandwiches," Dan said, grinning at Carrot.

Carrot started to relax.

"Nah," he said, holding up his hand. "Just kidding. They melted it down into oil for lanterns."

"Thanks, Dan. Kristine?"

The girl in front of her, with the red-rimmed glasses, turned around. "Hi," she said, smiling at Carrot.

"Hi." Carrot noticed that Kristine wore the same perfume as Beaut, something that smelled like apples.

"Well, uh, the guy, the harpooner—what's his name?—Queequeg, gets sick. Real sick and umm, he has the carpenter make him a coffin shaped like a canoe. Except that he doesn't die after all so he carves all kinds of weird designs on the canoe. And, umm—" She poked up her glasses with her finger. "Oh, yeah, then there's this really bad storm, and lightning hits the three masts and sets them on fire and all the men know it's a bad sign. All the men except Ahab. He thinks he's God."

"Does he?" Mrs. Smoznak asked.

"Yeah," several kids said.

"No," some other kids said.

"Well, let's read on and find out," Mrs. Smoznak said,

picking up the book. "Carrot, do you have any questions before I continue?"

Carrot shook her head. She felt warm inside. They liked her. Everyone liked her. Maybe she wasn't a freak after all.

On the way out of class Mrs. Smoznak stopped her. "How did you like the book?"

"I liked it," Carrot said.

"Good. Here's an extra copy. You can read it over summer vacation." She handed Carrot the book.

To Carrot's relief she didn't mention a word about coming in during study hall to get makeup work. Carrot went off to her other classes feeling happier than she had in almost two months. Maybe she wouldn't love it at Peelee but at least she wouldn't hate it. Her English class had spent the whole hour helping introduce her to *Moby-Dick*. Nobody had treated her like a freak. They had made her feel important.

At lunch Carrot sat in her usual corner and made a little squared-off area on the Formica table with her lunch bag, her apple, her cookies, and the wrapper from her chicken sandwich. Usually no one sat with her, but if they did Carrot pretended to be doing homework; she opened a notebook and wrote out long rows of sevens while she ate so people would think she was a mathematical genius or something. But today she opened to the first page of *Moby-Dick*. "Call me Ishmael," she read. She closed the book. Ishmael was the narrator, she remembered—the teacher who became a harpooner. She wondered if Ahab ever got the great white whale. She took a bite of her sandwich and opened the book again.

"That's not a blubber sandwich, is it?"

Carrot looked up into the smiling dark eyes of the boy from her English class. "Oh, hi," she said, swallowing.

"Is your name really Carrot?" he asked. "Like rabbit food?"

She nodded. Then she added, "Well, it's Carrie." Then she added, "Well, it's Carissa."

"Next you're gonna tell me it's Carissamissa."

She put down her sandwich and laughed.

"My name's Dan Durbin."

"Oh, hi," she said again, stupidly. She wondered if he was going to sit down. No boy had ever just come up and sat with her at lunch before, not even in Regal.

"Hey," he said, putting both hands on the table and leaning toward her. "Are you really a squirrel killer?"

Carrot blinked. "H-huh?"

"I heard you're a great white squirrel-killer. But you don't look that savage. Hey—where you going?"

"I have to leave," she said, hastily packing up her lunch. And she did, without looking back.

6

*C*arrot was turning the handle of the food grinder as she pushed through hunks of stale bread, cabbage leaves, and carrots. The squiggly worms of garbage that came out the holes plopped into a big red bowl on a footstool under the grinder. Babe had told her the chickens wouldn't eat anything bigger than gravel, so it was her job to sort the day's leftovers into compost garbage and chicken garbage and grind up what the chickens would eat.

Gram was flouring her hands, getting ready to knead her lump of bread dough. At the other end of the room, under the moose head, her mother was fussing over Beaut's hair.

"I can't wear my hair pinned up, Mother. After three scissors kicks it would be flying all over. I don't want to end up looking like Lubella Whittier."

Lubella Whittier was a woman their mother sold Rainbow Makeup to back in Regal, whose hair stuck out all over like cotton candy.

"I just want to look normal, not wild, not boring, just like—like why not a ponytail or something?"

Carrot could tell Beaut was nervous about cheerleading tryouts. She wasn't usually so twitchy.

"Just let's try this," her mother said, lifting her hands under Beaut's hair and kind of bouncing it up and down to test the curl. "More curls around your face and the rest—" She stopped talking and began clipping pin curls across Beaut's forehead. Then she picked up a can of hair spray and sprayed all over Beaut's head for about twenty seconds. "Oooh," she exclaimed, sounding more excited than Carrot had heard her in months, "this will be so perfect. You'll look like an old-fashioned valentine."

"I don't know," Beaut said, flipping up the mirrored lid of Mom's Rainbow briefcase. "What do you think, Gram?"

"Oh, Gram doesn't know anything about hairstyles," her mother said.

"No, I do not," Gram said, stabbing a hairpin into her coiled braid. "Every day I thank my lucky stars that I have more important matters to contend with. When you get done hair spraying that moose head, Susan, you might carry the egg cartons out to Babe and send him in here before he leaves."

Carrot knew Gram was annoyed that her mom didn't do anything but fiddle with her hair or Beaut's hair and makeup. Sometimes she dusted the living room, but then she would stand at the mantel for an hour and rearrange her china shoe collection that she'd brought from home. She didn't contribute much to what Gram called "the care and feeding of five people."

"You look nice, Beaut," Carrot said, trying to smooth things over. "I know you'll make it."

Her mother looked up at Carrot. "I should think you

49

would want to go watch your sister's tryouts. It would give Beaut great encouragement to have you cheering her on."

"I have to—to feed the chickens," Carrot said lamely. She had no desire to go sit in the bleachers with a bunch of screaming weirdos all afternoon. "Beaut?" she asked uncertainly.

"It's okay, Care. I don't want anyone to be around. I'm too nervous."

Carrot picked up the bowl and headed for the door. "Good luck."

"Find a buck," Babe said, coming in with a basket of eggs.

Carrot and Beaut exchanged a look. "Good luck, find a buck," was what they used to say to their father when he went hunting. It had become a good-luck expression for everything from a math exam to Beaut's first date.

"Ah, Babe," Gram said quietly, wiping her floury hands on her apron. "Here, let me have a look at you." Gram was so tall she stood head to head with Babe when she took him by the shoulders and turned him toward the overhead light.

Carrot watched while Gram retied Babe's red bow tie, smoothed his hair, and tucked his hankie in the pocket of his black-and-white plaid sport coat. Gram could be a crabby old lady but with Babe she was as tender as Henny Penny. Carrot looked from Gram to her mother combing Beaut's hair. She turned and went out to feed the chickens.

While she was still in the chicken yard Babe went by on his bike, his basket full of egg cartons.

"Here I go, Carrot. Mr. Eggs is on his way." He kept

both hands on the handlebars, nodding wildly in farewell.

Carrot waved back and watched his wobbly progress down the rutted drive. Babe was a funny sight, his plaid coat whipping out behind him, his big rear end hanging over the bike seat. After he disappeared into the woods Carrot scattered the rest of the food across the yard, stepped over the squawking chickens, and closed the gate behind her. She didn't want to go back in the house. The day was warm and overcast. At the edge of the woods the heavy sweetness of lilacs floated on the air. Carrot walked toward the lavender and white sprigs, thinking she would pick them for Gram's table, but she kept walking till she got to a giant oak that stood alone in the clearing, its huge limbs just now sprouting green, long after the other trees had leafed. Carrot looked up. There were birds chittering in the branches—probably nests of sparrows. She touched the trunk with her finger, tracing the rough grooves of the bark. Then she put her arms around the tree, pressing her face against the scratchy trunk.

Closing her eyes, she thought about the day in her English class when it seemed that everyone liked her, wanted to be her friend. And that boy, Dan, coming up to her during lunch, all smiles and jokes and then calling her a squirrel killer. What a jerk—pretending to pal around and then making fun of her. And he wasn't the only one, either. Brenda, the blubber queen, with hair like saw grass, came over to her desk the next day. "Did you ever, like, shoot anything really, really sweet, like a bunny rabbit or a little fox?" Carrot wanted to jump up from her desk and stran-

51

gle her, but instead she opened *Moby-Dick* and turned to her marker in chapter two. But Brenda wouldn't let it go. She turned to Cindy and said, "She's like a big game hunter, like Ernest Hemingway or something. You'd better not let your dogs run loose."

Carrot had slammed her book shut. "Stuff it, fatso," she said, looking Brenda squarely in the face.

"Jeez," Brenda said. "It was only a joke. What a dork," she muttered. And she and Cindy went off to their seats, whispering and looking back over their shoulders at her.

Carrot stretched her arms wider around the tree, flattening herself against the trunk. Nothing could hurt a tree. It stayed the same through the wind and rain and snow, its roots deep and safe in the earth. How good it would be to be a big old oak tree, standing all alone in an empty field.

"Carrot?"

Carrot sprang back from the tree. It was Babe, straddling his bike, his egg cartons still in his basket as if he had never left. "Wh-what are you doing?" Carrot asked, embarrassed to be seen hugging a tree.

"I came back for you. Mr. Eggs came back for you," he corrected himself. "Come on," he said. "They give you cookies and their dogs lick your hand."

Carrot shook her head. "No way. I don't want to talk to anyone, Babe."

"You see," he said, raising a finger, "Carrot, you don't got to. You see, I do all the talking. I'm Mr. Eggs. You be my helper and stand back and don't say nothing. I give them the eggs. They say, 'Thank you very much, here's a dollar and a cookie.' And I say, 'Could I have one for my helper?' And they give it to me not to you. The people do what I ask. Just stand back and don't say nothing."

Carrot ran her fingers over the bark, back and forth, back and forth, until her fingertips tingled. She looked back at the house. Gram was baking bread. Beaut and Mom were probably going through her makeup case. Carrot had tons of homework in all of her classes but she was already so far behind that in the three weeks left she was never going to catch up anyway. She sighed, "Okay."

Carrot jogged down the drive beside Babe, who pedaled slowly because of all the ruts. Once they got out on Bentley they picked up a little speed, but it was an easy pace for Carrot. Beside her, Babe started to sing one of his Sunday school songs, "'Tis the gift to be simple, 'tis the gift to be free, 'tis the gift to come down, where you ought to be. . . ." She listened to her feet thudding against the gravel shoulder and the soft jiggling of the egg cartons in Babe's basket and, occasionally, the whish of a car going past into town. A breeze lifted the fragrance of sweet pea from the banks along either side of the road.

Babe stopped singing and pointed at the clearing ahead. "Ruby Dodd," he said. "She's a magic lady."

Carrot looked up, but just then a truck roared past, horn blaring. Two boys yelled through their open window as they went by, "Ba-a-a-by!"

Babe stopped pedaling and pulled off the road, watching till they were out of sight.

"Who was that?" Carrot asked.

"Dudley and Bert." Babe leaned forward and stroked the egg cartons as if to soothe them. "They don't like me."

Carrot couldn't imagine anyone disliking Babe. He was the gentlest person she knew. "Why not?"

"'Cause Gram reported them for shining deer on our land. They can't get a license no more."

"Creeps," Carrot said. She shook her head. "Dad hated deer shiners. When the deer freeze in their headlights it's like shooting ducks in a barrel. How can anybody do that?"

"I don't like them, neither," Babe muttered, dragging his bike back onto the paved shoulder of the road. "They always yell like that. 'Ba-a-a-by.' I'm not a baby. I'm Babe."

"Forget it, Babe. They're slimebags."

"Slimebags," he repeated, starting to pedal again.

Ruby Dodd's house was lavender, with purple shutters and flower boxes crammed with all colors of flowers. Across the front were painted purple and yellow moons, suns, crescents, and stars, like Ruby Dodd's house had fallen out of the sky.

Carrot leaned against the side of the house and held on to Babe's bike when he went up to deliver a carton of eggs. She heard a loud voice say, "Get in here, Mr. Eggs. I near gave up on my Denver omelet this morning, dad blast ya. You been out chasing frogs?"

Carrot was glad Ruby Dodd was friends with Babe. She hated people like Bert and Dudley who made fun of him. Her dad had always treated Babe like somebody better than a brother. "He's finer than your average," he always said of Babe. "He's got a heart bigger than the sun and a goodness that's deeper than Coomby Lake." Carrot knew that Babe was finer than average and that once he had saved her father's life. But people didn't know that about Babe. They thought because he wasn't as smart as other

54

people that he wasn't as good, either. And they didn't know how to take him. Sometimes Carrot saw people shout at him like he was deaf. Or they would talk about him when he was standing right there, as if he was a brick wall. Carrot could tell right away if she was going to like people by the way they treated Babe.

"So—who is this little fire bush hiding out here?" Ruby Dodd came outside and lifted Carrot's cap so that her hair tumbled down.

Babe laughed. "It's not a bush," he said. "It's Carrot."

"Well, cross me, it *is* a carrot," Ruby Dodd said, grinning at Carrot. "Or a tomato. You look good enough to eat, Missy. So here ya go." She held out a lumpy, powdery ball of fried dough.

What Ruby Dodd said didn't make much sense to Carrot. She took the warm doughnut and stared at the plump woman in long skirts. She wasn't as old as Gram because her hair was black as crows' feathers, and her round red cheeks were free from wrinkles. She had seashells around her neck, hundreds of them on strings, and they clacked against each other when she moved. Even her earrings were long chains of colored shells hanging all the way to her shoulders, and they jiggled and swung as Ruby Dodd laughed and tossed her head.

"Get on your way," she said, thumping Babe on the back. "Willie Finn will be blaming me for his French toast. You can tell him I took two eggs from his carton to pay me back. And tell him if he wants his tea read to come after my wash is on the line. Harmony, Carrot, harmony. Leave off hiding from the world."

Carrot blinked and stared at Ruby Dodd. Then she followed Babe out of the yard, looking back over her shoulder to see Ruby waving her doughnut, making an arc of powdered sugar in the air.

Ruby Dodd opened the star-painted door to her house, but before she went in she called, "Mind what I say about accidents, Babe. Have a care."

Carrot was so startled that she mashed the doughnut in her fist before she knew what she was doing. "How did she know I was there? Did you tell her, Babe?"

"Nope." Babe had shoved the entire doughnut in his mouth and was chewing furiously as he pedaled for the main road.

Carrot started to jog. "Maybe she saw me from the road."

Babe shook his head, licking powder from his lips. "Watch this," he said, unconcerned. He stood up and pedaled hard toward a thin plank covering a water-filled ditch. But at the last minute he stopped. "I don't wanna break my eggs," he explained, walking the bike over the plank. "Gotta be careful."

Carrot had never met anyone who could tell fortunes. At the road she looked back down into the green patch of yard where the lavender house nestled like an egg in an Easter basket. "Why?" she said to Babe. "Why did she tell you that?"

They had turned onto Bentley, in the direction of Willie Finn's house. "Because," Babe said simply.

But before either of them could say another word the blue truck came barreling up behind them, careening out onto the shoulder. Carrot felt a spray of gravel fly up into her face, striking her lips, her eyes, her cheeks. Beside her Babe hollered and went over, his bike under him. Cartons of eggs flew up and then down, scrambling eggs all over the road.

7

*G*ram called the police.

"Now, don't go making trouble, Clara," Carrot's mother said, the crease between her eyes deepening. "I just know those boys didn't know what they were doing."

"Those boys are eighteen and nineteen years old and if they want to play games, they'd best not do it with my children and a ten-ton truck. I'll see them behind bars first."

Sitting at the kitchen table with Babe, still shaken from what had happened, Carrot knew Gram was right. It hadn't been a mistake. The boys had wanted to hurt them. They were glad she and Babe had fallen and broken all the eggs. They were probably still laughing.

Together, she and Babe told the police officer what had happened, how Bert and Dudley Horning sped by the first time, yelling at Babe, and how they returned fifteen minutes later and knocked Babe off his bike, breaking all the eggs.

"How many?" the officer asked.

"F-five," Babe said, wringing his hands.

"Five dozen," Gram said.

"Would you like them to pay for damages?" the officer asked.

"Heavens, no," Carrot's mother said.

"Yes," Gram said, signing the report the officer held out to her. "Five dollars," she said. "Payable to Babe Turvy."

After the police officer left, Gram started banging around in the kitchen, slamming cupboard doors, rattling a spoon around in a mixing bowl so hard it made Carrot's ears ring. Carrot took the peas Gram asked her to shell and went around the counter and sat on the floor under the moose. She split open the first pod and scooped out four fat peas and popped them in her mouth. She chomped down so that the peas burst open and she tasted spring. Every year Gram's first crop was peas and she always sent bagfuls home with Carrot and her dad. For weeks they ate peas with every meal. But, best of all, Carrot liked them raw, fresh and green, right from the pod.

After ten minutes her mother came into the living room. "Have you seen my bottle of Peachy Ice?" she asked, looking under the wicker lamp table.

Carrot shook her head and scrunched forward so her mother could look on top of the mantel.

"It's no wonder you slouch," she said, pausing to frown down at Carrot. "You can't shell peas like that." She moved over to the sofa and started lifting the cushions. "I just wish you hadn't caused such a big ruckus today. My nerves are all atwitter. I'm going to have to take some aspirin. And I can't stop thinking about Beaut. Will she make it? Won't she make it? This means everything to her.

59

It means the difference between being accepted and just being on the fringe. And after what we've been through, some good news would certainly be welcome. Well, you know Beaut, she'll make the best of whatever happens but—really Carrot, must you sit right in the middle of the floor?"

Carrot sighed and picked up the bowl and the bag of peas. She walked past Gram, who was greasing two muffin pans, and went out the back door. It was raining so she walked around the back of the house and over to the chicken coop. When she stepped inside she stood there for a moment letting her eyes adjust to the darkness, strangely comforted by the acrid odor, blended with the smell of dust and fresh straw. She glanced in Henny Penny's box and smiled to see Henny Penny's sharp little eyes watching her. All the chicks were running around the pen peeping and climbing on top of one another. They were starting to get real feathers that looked like glossy orange paint against their soft down. Pretty soon they could go outside just like the big chickens.

Carrot started for the corner where Babe kept some bales of clean straw. Then she stopped. Babe was sitting in the corner with his head pressed against the wall.

"Babe," she whispered.

Babe didn't move.

She came closer. "Are you okay, Babe?" She reached out and touched his shoulder.

Without turning, Babe shook his head.

Suddenly Carrot was afraid. Babe was having a heart

attack. He had come out to the shed to die. "I'll run and get Gram."

"No, Carrot, no, no, no."

Babe turned around and Carrot saw that he had been crying. She had never seen a man cry before. But then she remembered that Babe wasn't really a man. He was a kid like her. Only younger.

"Are you sick, Babe?"

He shook his head. "It's my head," he said, pointing between his eyes. "There's something wrong in here."

Carrot sat on a straw bale beside him. "What is it?"

"I don't know," he said hoarsely. "Carrot, I don't know." He hung his head and looked at his hands. "I'm not like other people," he said. "I'm cracked."

"No—"

"Cracked, cracked, cracked," he said, striking his forehead with his fist and starting to rock back and forth.

Carrot didn't know what to say. She knew if she went for Gram, *she* would know how to make Babe feel better. But that would be like giving up on him. "Babe, I don't think you're cracked."

"Yes you do," he whispered, still not looking at her.

She stared at him, a grown man in a red bow tie and a plaid sport coat, rocking back and forth on a bale of straw. "You're different," she said slowly. "But you're not cracked. You know everything about chickens. You know how much to feed them and how to get them to lay eggs. You raised twelve little chicks all by yourself. And look how much Henny Penny trusts you. She won't let anyone but you touch her chicks."

Babe lifted his head. "Bert and Dudley made me break all my eggs. They think I'm a big baby."

"Bert and Dudley are slimebags. They don't know the first thing about raising chickens. Everybody in this whole town knows Mr. Eggs. They know you have the best eggs in Peelee."

Babe nodded soberly.

"They're bullies, Babe. Trying to pick a fight from a ten-ton truck. And shooting poor defenseless deer after they shined them. *They're* cracked, Babe, not you. You would never do something like that."

"I would never," Babe vowed. "I would never shine a deer. I would never drive a truck into someone and break all their eggs." He shook his head. "I would never put a killed deer in a wheelbarrow and run it down Main Street. They did that, Carrot, one time. And it was a sorry sight, that deer all crumpled up like a baby doll. And them laughing and laughing. I saw it on my bike and I told them, 'Turn around and git home with the deer. It's not to laugh over.' And they—they—" Babe stopped. "They did something," he whispered, hanging his head.

Carrot stood up. "What?" she asked sharply, her cheeks burning in anger at the desecration of the deer.

Babe shook his head. "I just don't wanna say it."

She put her hand on his shoulder. "What was it, Babe? You can tell me."

"They made me a fool again," he murmured. After a long pause he told her. "They cut off the deer's tail and pinned it to my—to my trousers where I couldn't get it off."

Carrot jumped up, her hands in tight fists. "Those jerk-faces—" She kicked the side of the shed, scattering the peas in the bowl all over the straw.

Babe gasped. "You don't supposed to—"

"Babe, didn't you fight them? Didn't you knock their stupid faces in?"

He shook his head. "Mama told me don't fight anybody. I'm gonna hurt somebody 'cause I'm too big. And I'm—you know—I'm cracked."

"Shut up, Babe. You're not cracked." Carrot sat down again on the straw bale, picturing Dudley and Bert breezing away in their blue truck, leaving her and Babe on top of his bike in a jumble of broken eggs. "Those creeps are going to pay for this," she said.

Babe nodded. "Five dollars. They hafta—"

"No," she said. "More than that. They have to suffer like they made you suffer. We'll think of something."

"We could burn their house down."

She sighed. "Get real, Babe. Do you want us to end up in jail?"

"We could put snakes in their bathtub. I seen that once at the movies. You see, the lady woke up and there was a bazillion of green snakes in her bathtub. We could do that—would that be okay?"

"I don't know, Babe. Maybe snakes. Maybe something else. Let's think."

Babe spit in his right hand and hammered it with his fist. "Good luck is coming. Spit in your hand, Carrot, and say, good luck is coming."

Just as Carrot spit in her hand they heard the clanging of the triangle at the corner of the house. Usually Gram rang it when Carrot's dad got a deer or it was someone's birthday.

When Carrot and Babe came out and looked around the corner they saw Gram and Mom hugging Beaut and they knew good luck had at least come to Beaut.

8

It was the last day of May and the hottest. Carrot and Babe worked together under the noonday sun, trying to finish the spring planting before nightfall. They had planted the seeds earlier—corn, carrots, radishes, beets, lettuce, beans, and squash. But two hundred green plants stretched out behind them in the shade of the maples, like a display from a garden store.

"This is going to take all weekend," Carrot groaned, flopping down next to the tomatoes. Her back ached from bending over, and sweat pasted her shorts and T-shirt to her body. She propped herself up on her elbows and took a long drink from the water bottle, letting some of the water splash over her face. She held up the bottle. "You want a drink?"

Babe shook his head without looking up from the pepper plants he was lifting from milk cartons and tucking into the soil. All the other years her father had helped him plant the big garden, and Carrot knew Babe was worried about messing it up. He wiped his dirty hands on his jeans.

"Did you check the p-pichur, Carrot, about the p-peppers?"

She held up the big layout Gram had done of the entire garden, including the cornfield, with all the rows written out in her big, sprawling handwriting. Gram had also put markers at the end of each row, labeled "tomatoes," "carrots," "cukes," so they would know exactly where a new row started. Some things Gram was pretty casual about but gardening wasn't one of them. She started planting hundreds of seeds while there was still snow on the ground, putting them in big wooden boxes that she lined up on wobbly old card tables along the living room windows. That was one of the reasons her mother had never liked going to Gram's. "It's filthy," she complained. "There's dirt all over the place." But it was only under the six living room windows and on the deep, low bathroom window ledge where it was warm and moist.

When the plants were big enough Gram and Babe transferred them to cold frames outside—dirt boxes with glass covers that would let in sunlight but protect the plants from freezing. And then, finally, sometime in May, the plants went into the garden. The huge garden supplied them with fresh vegetables all summer and fall and canned vegetables the rest of the year. Besides that, Babe sold produce from a roadside stand. Gram's garden isn't just a hobby the way it is for people back in Regal, Carrot thought. Nobody in Regal had a garden this big.

She sat up and hugged her knees, watching Babe with his little stick measuring the space between plants, digging a tidy little hole with the blue spade, dropping in the bright green plant and tamping the dirt down with his thick hands. So careful, she thought, afraid he would make a mistake. Unlike her father who scooped out a hole, dropped in a plant, scooped out another hole, dropped in a plant, knowing just what he was doing without thinking about it for a second. She leaned back against the maple tree and squinted over at Babe, watching his bulk blur and shimmer between her lashes. The way his black hair fell over his face when he bent over was just like her father. And there, just how he swatted at a mosquito on the back of his neck. It was exactly, exactly her father—even to the way he swiped his arm across his forehead to wipe off the sweat.

As she watched her heart leaped into her throat. It really *was* her father sitting there on the freshly tilled earth. He had sprung back up to life like one of Gram's plants. In one more second he would see her sitting there with her heart as big as the sun. And he would throw back his head and laugh and grab her and dance her over the grass. No, she thought, changing her mind. At first he would be very stern. He would mention the terrible report card sitting on the kitchen table. He would lift one black eyebrow and look down at her with his arms crossed and say, like he always did, "How can somebody so smart be so dumb?" But he couldn't stay mad, not after being gone so long. In another instant he would start that slow smile and reach out to her. He would say—

"Carrot, you promised. You promised to help me."

Carrot's eyes squeezed shut against Babe's voice. She took a deep breath. "I'm coming, Babe," she said. "I was just—" She got up, not finishing the sentence. Just acting out a stupid little play, she thought, walking back to the garden, blinking back tears.

She picked up the other trowel and took some of the pepper plants and started digging next to Babe.

"Hi, Carrot," he said, a big smile spreading across his dirt-streaked face.

"What are you so cheerful about?" she snapped, tearing away a milk carton.

"This is yours and mine garden—just the two of us."

"Yeah, well I think Gram is going to make us share it."

"But, you see, it's just you and me making this. Like an important project. Like an a-a-assignment."

"Whoopee," Carrot said.

"Don't you get it, Carrot? We're making food for everyone. Just like Jesse. Only it'll be us this time."

Carrot smacked the dirt down with both hands. "We're frying up out here while they're inside drinking lemonade." She knew that wasn't true. Beaut was in town, applying for a job at Lisanne's Lingerie, and Gram was baking strawberry rhubarb muffins in the hot kitchen. If anyone was drinking lemonade it was her mother. Carrot wondered if she had looked at her report card yet. "I guess I'm better off out here, anyway," she said to Babe. "Once I go inside Mom's going to bite my head off."

"Did you break something?" Babe asked, no doubt remembering how he got yelled at for shattering two of her mom's china shoes when he reached up to put Mr. Eggs's money in a crock on the mantel.

"No," Carrot said. "I got two C's and four D's."

"Is that bad?" Babe handed her another plant.

"Yeah. One time Dad wouldn't let me come to Gram's for a whole month because I got a D in math. He was furious."

"Are you stupid, Carrot?" Babe lifted his head to look at her.

She shrugged. "I didn't do any homework. Didn't even open a book. Not since—since March. You could call that stupid."

Babe nodded. "Mr. Eggs always does his homework. Like I never forget to feed the chickens and I clean the coop and Mr. Eggs delivers the eggs Saturday, Tuesday, and Thursday. And I put my money in the jar."

"So you're saying I'm stupid and you're smart. Thanks a lot, Babe." She smacked him in the chest, leaving a dirty handprint on his T-shirt.

"Naw, Carrot." Babe ducked his head and looked embarrassed.

But Carrot shook her head. "Some friend. Make me feel bad, why don't you?"

They got all the tomatoes and peppers in and Carrot was walking along the rows with a sprinkling can when Beaut called them in for dinner.

By the time Babe and Carrot had washed up, Beaut, Gram, and Mom were already at the table, discussing Beaut's new job.

"Did you hear, Carrie?" her mother asked, reaching across the table to remove Carrot's cap. "Beaut has a job selling at Lisanne's, making four-fifty an hour. Her first grown-up job. Can you believe it?"

"Yup," Carrot said, digging into the potatoes. She knew Beaut would get the job. Things always fell into place for her. Beaut was not only pretty, she was nice. Already she had a new boyfriend and as many friends as she had had back in Regal. She had made the cheerleading team and now she had a job. Carrot felt a stab of envy.

"I'm going to put half of it in the money jar, Gram. To help with expenses. I know things have gotten tight since we moved in."

Carrot thought she was going to puke. Why did she have to have this angelic sister? "Nice going, Beaut," Carrot said, without looking up. "I bet you even got a perfect report card, didn't you?"

"Not really." Beaut poured herself a glass of milk. "I got a B in geometry."

"Awww," Carrot said, her voice heavy with sarcasm. She waited for her mother to say something about *her* report card, but she only reached across the table and pushed Carrot's hair off her forehead.

"I'm glad you wear that silly old cap out in the hot sun. It keeps your hair bright as a new penny."

Carrot looked across at her mother in her blue satin robe. "Did you see my report card?"

Her mother sighed. "Yes, I suppose I did. It was on the table, wasn't it?"

"It was all C's and D's," Carrot said. "Mostly D's."

Her mother shook her head. "That's terrible, Carrie." Then she turned back to Beaut. "Does that twenty-percent discount apply to everything in the store, even the—"

"I got a D in English, a D in social studies, a D in home ec, and a D in math."

70

"Well, you really ought to try harder," her mother said, squeezing lemon into her tea.

"You don't care!" Carrot said hotly.

"Now calm down, Carrie. You should be happy I'm so easy on you. It's just that I have other things on my mind."

"What do you have on your mind? Gram does all the cooking and cleaning; Babe takes care of the chickens. Beaut has a job. Babe and I planted the garden—"

"All b-by ourselves," Babe said.

"What do you ever do but stick dumb flowers in your hair and put on makeup and take it off again? You don't even get dressed. You walk around in that stupid robe like you just got out of the hospital."

"That's enough." Gram reached over and put her hand over Carrot's.

"*No!*" Carrot said. "You act like you're the only one who's hurt. Like you're walking around with this humongous broken heart. That's just a big crock and everyone knows it. If you had loved Dad so much why didn't you want him to be happy? You never wanted him to go hunting, you thought he was a slob, you nagged him to make more money. You ruined it for him, that's what you did." Carrot picked up her napkin and blew her nose. "You ruined everything." Without looking at anyone she got up from the table and ran upstairs.

She sat on the edge of her bed and listened to the noises from downstairs. Her mother was probably bawling her head off and Beaut was trying to make her feel better, telling her that she had been a wonderful wife, a wonderful mother.

"Manure," Carrot said. She went to the mirror and

71

looked at her red-rimmed eyes, her tangled hair. Opening the pie safe, she found the scissors. Before she could change her mind she grabbed a big wad of hair and cut it off.

9

C arrot woke up the first time Jupiter crowed. She looked over at her sister but Beaut didn't even budge. Now she slept right through until the alarm woke her. Carrot climbed out of bed and stood in front of the crackly mirror trying to see her hair. It was too dark. All she could see was this shadowy figure with jagged pieces of hair on either side of her face. The Grim Reaper. That was a painting in her social studies book of a skinny man with spiky hair and a curved blade. She reached on top of the pie safe for her cap. It felt too big without all her hair stuffed up inside.

Gram was downstairs drinking coffee and cutting out a cheerleading skirt on the kitchen table. She was making all the skirts and bow ties for Beaut's team. Sewing was a way Gram made extra money.

"Morning," Gram said, glancing up. "You're awake early."

Carrot nodded and sat down.

"Coffee?" Gram never offered her coffee when her

mother was around. Carrot had started drinking it years ago, from a thermos, when she and her dad were out in the blind on frosty mornings; and Gram would also fix it for her at Sunday breakfasts, loaded with cream and sugar. That's how she fixed it now and set it under Carrot's nose.

"Thanks, Gram."

"You upset your mother last night," Gram said, unpinning the paper from the blue fabric and sticking the pins in her mouth.

Carrot took off her cap and waited for Gram to look at her.

Gram gasped and the pins fell out, making a little ticking dance across the table. "Well," she said at length. She pulled out a chair and sat down, looking into Carrot's face. "Did you want to hurt your mother this much?"

Carrot hung her head. "Yes—no. I—she—she's so selfish, Gram. All she thinks about is herself. She's like some great dramatic actress parading around all day in her nightgown, never thinking of anyone else. I was the one who loved him, Gram. Not her. All they ever did was fight."

Gram stiffened. "Now aren't *you* the one being selfish?"

Carrot looked at Gram's long, wrinkled face, with the gray braid hanging on one side. She recognized her father's gesture as Gram rubbed her thumb between her eyebrows. Gram had lost her son.

"Oh, Gram," she said, covering her face with her hands. "I keep saying the wrong things and doing the wrong things. I don't want to talk about it but then I do want to talk about it. How can I not talk about the worst thing in the whole world? It's so awful, I know it can't be true. I keep thinking

74

he's here, he's just out in the garden or chopping firewood. Because I know, I just know, he can't be—"

"Dead," Gram said. She leaned over and put her arm around Carrot. "I feel the same."

"You do?"

"And so does your mother. Some worse, maybe. Because they did argue. Damn guilt will eat your guts out."

Carrot took a sip of coffee and held the sweetness and the bitterness in her mouth for a moment, thinking of Sunday mornings, her father's whiskery face, the smell of maple syrup, and the old black radio crackling with the weather behind them in the living room.

Gram stood up. "We'd best fix that hair." She pulled a thinner pair of scissors from the drawer—the ones she trimmed Babe's hair with. Draping a blue dish towel around Carrot's shoulders she snipped a little bowl all around her face.

By the time Mr. Eggs was ready Carrot had clipped her hair back and hidden it under the John Deere cap.

"C'mon, Carrot," Babe said, trying to stand still while Gram tied his red bow tie. "We don't want to be late." He looked at Gram. "I turned on the sprinklers, Mama."

Gram took his face between her big veiny hands and kissed him. "Ah, Babe, I don't know what we'd all do without a man to take care of us."

She caught Carrot on her way out the door and kissed the top of her cap. "And you behave yourself," she said.

Carrot put her arms around Gram, laying her face against the sturdy bosom, breathing in the aroma of cinnamon. Then she ran out after Babe's bike.

As they moved down the drive Carrot thought of all the

things they had to do that day. "Think we'll get the rest of the plants in?"

"Yup," Babe said, not taking his eyes off the ruts in the drive.

"I want to get back to *Moby-Dick*."

"Who's that?"

"It's not a who. It's a book from my English class." Carrot hadn't told anyone about the note Mrs. Smoznak had stuck in with her report card. And she didn't exactly know why she had made up her mind to read such a long book, except that Mrs. Smoznak's note gave her a warm feeling.

Dear Carrot,

I'll be thinking about you over the summer, walking around in your grandmother's woods. Why don't you curl up under a tree and read *Moby-Dick* and turn in a book report in the fall? That way I can change your D. Because you're not a D, Carrot. You're much better than that. Remember, "When you get to the end of your rope, tie a knot and hang on."

Yours fondly,
Mrs. Smoznak

When they got out on Bentley Carrot said, "It's about a whale."

"What?" Babe squinted at her in the sunlight.

"*Moby-Dick*," she said. "It's about this guy—"

"Ba-a-beeee!"

They heard the voices before they heard the truck and they both headed for the ditch. But the blue truck sailed on by without swerving, the laughter of the Horning boys flying back in their faces.

"Are you okay?"

Carrot looked at Babe who was hunched under a tree, his arms over his head, like the sky had fallen in on him. Babe lowered his arms and looked out at the road. He was breathing hard and his eyes were round with fear. "Are they coming?"

She shook her head, too furious to speak. She was still holding on to Babe's handlebar, which she had caught when he jumped for the ditch. She dragged the bike up and started stomping down the road. "Spider spit!" she yelled, but the truck had long disappeared. "Slimebags," she said to Babe. "Lily-livered slimebags. I'm going to kill them with my bare hands if I ever see them again." She kicked furiously at a stone and sent it bouncing down the road. "Like we're a coupla tin cans or something. Like they can just take potshots at us. Those BB brains, those dorking nitwit monkey-faced wartheads."

Babe just lumbered along beside her, wringing his hands and whimpering.

When they got to Ruby Dodd's Carrot was still so mad that she couldn't sit quietly and wait for Babe. She walked around and around a huge weeping willow in the front yard, pulling off branches and switching the ground with them as she walked. Before long Ruby Dodd came out the door with Babe and a small gray goat. She held a plate of corn bread.

"Aren't gonna sting me, are ya?" she called from her porch.

Carrot stopped pacing and looked at her, her shiny purple skirts sweeping the porch boards. Had Babe told her she was upset or was Ruby using magic?

"Girl." Ruby Dodd motioned her forward.

Carrot walked out from under the tree toward the porch.

"You got to live in the light, little friend."

Carrot stared at her, waiting for more. Ruby Dodd didn't make any sense. If she was going to give advice, why didn't she tell them what to do about the Horning boys?

Ruby Dodd tipped her head to one side. "I hear your little worry song." She tipped her head to the other side and started to sing, her voice as raspy as a saw on a tree limb. "I'm carrying a bucketful of my own tears and I cain't go on, cain't go on, cain't go on." She stopped. "Yes, you can go on, Carrot. Ya won't like the killin' part but you'll go on. You'll let go of that bucket, too." Putting her arm around the goat she sat on the steps and held out the plate of corn bread. Carrot shook her head.

On the way out to the road Carrot kept looking back at Ruby Dodd's house to see if there was a rainbow over it or glitter dust—something that made Ruby Dodd so strange. The purple house covered with moons and stars wasn't exactly ordinary-looking, but that didn't explain Ruby Dodd's magic—if it was magic.

She turned to Babe and when she spoke her voice trembled. "What did she mean, Babe, by—by the killing part?"

"The killing part?" Babe considered this as if she had asked him what tomorrow's weather would be. "Somebody's gonna get killed."

"Don't say that," Carrot pleaded.

Babe finished his corn bread and licked his fingers. He got back on his bike and started pedaling toward Willie Finn's house. "Once she found my little boat from the Jewel Tea man. Ruby Dodd told me, 'Look under the Slagels' mailbox.' I went back there and I found it sitting there on the ground, waiting for me."

"Stupid," Carrot said, changing her mind. "People can't see four miles away." But she thought about her bucket of tears. Was that the terrible heaviness she had been carrying around day after day? And she thought about the killing part. "Stupid," she said again. But that didn't stop her from feeling creepy.

After they had delivered the last two cartons of eggs to Mrs. Spring, who lived down a dirt road, they were turning back onto Bentley when Carrot stopped jogging. "Babe," she grabbed his arm and pointed through the underbrush. "Look at that truck."

Babe stopped and stared. "It's them. Let's get outta here."

"Wait," she whispered. "They're not around, are they?" They both looked in all directions. "I have this great idea," Carrot said out loud. "Stay here and keep watch." She started working her way through the trees to where the truck was parked.

"No, Carrot," Babe called after her, "come back."

But Carrot stopped only long enough to pluck a small screwdriver from the pocket of her jacket. When she got to the truck she dropped on her hands and knees and crawled, moving from tire to tire, until she had let the air out of all four.

When she got back Babe was sitting on a stump with his eyes closed. He was saying, "Now I layme down to sleep, now I layme down to sleep, now I layme—"

Carrot laughed. "Hey, Babe, it's okay. Let's get out of here. They'll never catch us on those tires." She started jogging beside Babe again. "Those turkeys. I'd love to see their stupid faces when they get back to the truck. They'll have to—" She stopped. "Hey, Babe."

Babe shook his head and kept pedaling.

"I know where they are!" She punched Babe's shoulder. "I know where they are! You know the gravel pit at the other side of Vestibini Road? That's where they are. They're swimming."

"Let's get away before they get back." Babe glanced back at the truck and pedaled harder.

"No!" Carrot laughed and jumped up and down. "I've got the greatest idea. Wait up, Babe." She ran after him and yanked on his jacket till he stopped. "I know exactly which way they went from the truck. I'm going to follow them down there. And when I find them you know what I'm going to do?"

Babe looked at her, wild eyed.

"I'm going to steal their clothes." She exploded into giggles.

"But, C-Carrot, don't d-do that. W-what if they catch you?"

"They won't. I know right where they are. I'll be back in a flash." She started back into the woods at a diagonal from the truck, ducking branches and jumping fallen logs. The foliage was thick and green but there was a path of sorts that had been beaten down over the years from all the people who had gone to the gravel pit to swim. She heard their voices before she came to the clearing. Quickly she dropped on her knees and crawled the last fifty feet and peeked around the bushes. What she was looking for was just ahead under a tree—Dudley and Bert's clothes. She craned her neck further and she could see one of them sitting buck naked on the shore, drinking a can of beer, and the other in the water, splashing at his brother with the palm of his hand. If she had a stick she could pull the clothes to her without being seen. She started crawling to a fallen log when she heard branches breaking behind her. Before she could move Babe appeared, looking like a frightened bear.

"Carrot," he said.

"Shhhh." She motioned for him to get down.

Babe squatted. "Carrot," he said, louder than before.

She couldn't waste another second. She dove forward, snatched up the clothes and darted back behind the bush. Her heart was thudding in her ears. "Did they see me?" she whispered. They sat there for a full minute but all they could hear was one of the boys yodeling—"odleodleodleodle la-hee-hoo."

They went back the way they had come, running and darting like jackrabbits. When they got back to the road, Carrot was as jittery as Babe. She dumped the clothes and shoes into Babe's basket and started running. "Let's go, Babe. Make tracks."

Babe started pedaling uphill like a wild man, looking over his shoulder every few seconds. "Opleaseopleaseopleaseo—" he said under his breath.

At the top of the hill Carrot started to laugh. "What are

we so worried about? They're not going to come after us. They haven't got any clothes. Can you see them, Babe, running down the highway stark—" She broke into a fit of giggles.

Babe just kept pedaling.

"Babe," she said, pulling him over. "They're naked as two little babies. They can't run around in broad daylight." Picturing Bert and Dudley running down the road bare naked, as mad as two hornets, she doubled over with laughter.

Babe still looked worried.

"Come on, Babe. They deserve it. Those fatheads."

He started to smile. "I was so scared, Carrot, I was so scared I said my prayers. But you're not afraid of anything." He looked at her with shining eyes. "You're the best, Carrot."

Carrot laughed and punched him in the arm and they started down the hill toward home.

10

"You're going to have to tell her sooner or later," Gram said, handing Carrot a tray with a cup and a chipped teapot on it. Before they moved in Gram had used the teapot to hold pencils. It was white china with a faded picture on it of a little purple house sitting on a patch of pink grass. Babe had painted it at the Sunday school Gram took him to every week.

"One of these nights she's going to pull your cap off at the table and another dinner will be ruined for everyone."

"Will she be mad, do you think?" Carrot knew the answer. She stood on one bare foot, nervously rubbing the back of her leg with the other.

"Just don't start bellowing like a sick cow up there. Be contrite, if you know how. And one more thing—she has a special favor to ask you. Make up your mind right now to be agreeable. It'll go easier on all of us if you say yes for a change."

Carrot started to ask what it was but then changed her mind. Gram didn't play games. If she had wanted to tell her she would have. She went upstairs with the tray and thumped the bottom of her mother's door with her foot, a sense of dread hanging over her. She hadn't exchanged more than a few words with her mother since the big scene at the dinner table.

"Oh, my," her mother said, clasping her hands under her chin. "Room service." She stood aside and pointed to the white wicker table beside her bed, then hurried over to it to move all the clutter of nail polish and makeup.

After Carrot had set the tray down she turned to her mother and gave her a weak smile. "You look nice, Mom." It was only after she said it that she realized it was true. Her mother was wearing a simple cotton sundress and she hadn't yet put her makeup on. With her hair pulled back in a ponytail and her scrubbed face, she looked like a real person instead of a lady in Hudson's Aisles of Beauty.

"I've been busy making lists," her mother said, waving a pad of paper under Carrot's nose. "You know what a list maker I've always been. I feel inspired, I feel like doing something again. And, Carrie, I have you to thank."

Carrot winced. "Mom, I—"

"No, no, no," her mother waved her words away. "I deserved every lash. I've been a terrible mother lately, a wretch really. I don't know how you all put up with me, walking around in my bathrobe, not lifting a single, solitary finger to help out."

"Well, you were upset," Carrot said, falling back on the old excuse her mother always offered whenever she was in one of her moods.

"I could drift around in my bathrobe the rest of my life and that wouldn't change a thing."

Carrot almost smiled. It sounded so much like Gram.

"So I'm going to go back to work. I'm ready to be a responsible person again, Carrie." She sat down on the edge of the bed and beamed up at Carrot. "And I need your help."

A little warning flag went up behind Carrot's eyeballs, but she smiled at her mother, not wanting to dampen her spirits.

"First I want you to know Gram has already agreed to do this. And if Gram, at her age, can be one of my models, I guess you can, too."

Carrot snorted. "Gram?" She pictured her grandmother with her frizzy gray braid and her jeans and clompy boots sitting primly while her mother swirled colored capes around her shoulders and dusted green powder on her eyelids.

"I'm going to have a Rainbow party right here downstairs in the big room with some of Gram's friends and neighbors, and we'll bake some lovely tea cookies and it will give us a chance to make new friends and to earn a little money at the same time." She rushed on, "Beaut will be my spring, of course, and Gram is a winter and you—it will only be this once, Carrie—but you're a perfect—" She stood up and pulled off Carrot's cap. Her face went slack and a sound escaped her lips—like a little squeak. Then she dropped to the bed.

Carrot sighed. "It'll grow, Mom."

Her mother stared up at Carrot without speaking. All her energy seemed to have floated out the window. Finally she said dully, "You did this to spite me."

"It's *my* hair," Carrot said. But she couldn't deny it. It

was the one thing about Carrot that her mother had always loved. Her "crimson bonnet," she called it in her flowery descriptions to her friends.

Carrot turned her back on her mother's expressionless gaze and looked out the window. She could see Babe in his John Deere cap digging between the tomato plants. He was talking to Henny Penny who was squatting in the dirt next to him. Babe had been digging up worms from the garden and feeding them to her by hand because she had been out of sorts lately, not laying and barely eating. At the edge of the garden next to Babe was Bing, her tin deer, also wearing a red John Deere cap and the red T-shirt she had taken from the Horning boys. On Bing's feet were Dudley and Bert's four sneakers. Even now Carrot wanted to laugh when she looked at Bing. Behind her she heard her mother sigh, and she turned around.

"I'll do it, Mom. I'll do the makeup thing if you want me to."

Her mother shook her head. "Your hair."

"But you can make it look good." She took the hair clips out and brushed it forward with her fingers. "That's what you're best at, Mom. Look, can't you put curls in it or something?"

"Why, Carrie?"

Carrot pretended not to know what she meant. "Why what?"

"Just tell me."

Carrot shrugged. "I was mad about—it sounds stupid but I wanted you to yell about my report card—to care, you know? It's like you know Beaut will be wonderful and I'll

86

always be the slug, so why bother to get upset over my lousy grades."

"You're jealous of Beaut? Oh, don't be silly, Carrie."

"I'm not silly." Carrot stamped her foot. "Dad didn't think I was silly. He thought I was smart and funny and that I tried hard. He said I—I had a deep feeling for things."

Carrot swallowed, remembering the day, years ago, when her father had said it. They had found a little speckled fawn curled up by a dead doe, its nose nuzzled against her blank face with its staring, gumdrop eyes. Carrot and her father had walked to within ten feet of the fawn and it barely moved, only lifting its head to look at them out of startled eyes.

Carrot clutched at her father's arm. "It isn't even afraid of us," she whispered.

"It *is* afraid, Carrot. It's just too weak to run away. Poor little guy probably hasn't eaten in a couple days."

Carrot was overcome with sorrow. She felt in her pockets and pulled out a blueberry muffin. "I'm going to give him this, Dad. Will he take it do you think? Maybe he'll eat right out of my hand."

The little fawn hunkered down closer to its mother when Carrot approached, and didn't even sniff at the muffin that she left on the mossy ground in front of it.

"It's still nursing," her father said. "It's a mite little for solid food."

A great surge of love rose up in her for the little abandoned deer. "We can give it some milk at Gram's until it can eat real food. We can make it strong in no time, Dad."

Her father shook his head. "We're going home this afternoon, Carrot. Gram doesn't need the extra work."

"Then let's take it back to our house and keep it in the backyard. We can make a little shelter behind the garage." She was suddenly desperate to save the fawn. "Oh, please, Dad—"

He just looked down at her, not saying a word. The idea was so ridiculous. A deer in Hightower Subdivision, surrounded by rose-covered picket fences and a sea of television antennas.

"Just for a little while. Until it gets strong enough to live on its own. I'd spend all my spare time with it, Daddy. Nobody else would have to do a thing, honest."

"Your mother would, Carrot. She would be kept from her roses. You know she would never set foot in the yard if there was a deer back there." He put his arm around her and drew her away from the clearing, back into the woods.

Carrot looked back over her shoulder and saw the fawn lift its head and watch her through the new leaves. She felt a pain in her heart so intense it took her breath away. All she could think about was the fawn shivering through the long chilly night waiting for its mother to come to life. "No!" She broke away from her father and ran back through the trees. Kneeling down she put both hands on the trembling back of the fawn. "I won't leave it to die. I won't. I'll stay here and die myself. You're mean, Daddy. I hate you. I hate you."

Her father came back and sat on a fallen log and watched her sobbing over the spotted fawn. Even now she could picture him in his buff-colored jacket, his big body slumped forward, arms resting on his knees, the brightness of spring all around him like a green halo. She could feel on her cheeks the faint breeze blowing through the scrub oaks. And the silence. Not a bird calling nor a bee droning. Just that little stirring of the breeze. She remembered it like a photograph—her, the speckled fawn, and the dead doe, and over there on the log, her father, bigger and stronger and better than anything in the woods.

Finally he spoke to her. "Carrot, over the years, I've spilled a lot of blood. Maybe a hundred times, a thousand times. And yet, no matter how many deer I shoot, how many pheasants or rabbits, it pulls at my heartstrings. Each time I wonder, how much better am I than this beautiful creature that I snuffed out of existence? Maybe, in the final judgment, someone's going to add up all the animals I've killed and say I'm liable for them. It makes me a little uneasy. Just like you, Carrot, death makes me uneasy. I've spent so much time in these woods I feel someways related to these damn critters. And you got the same wildness in you, Carrot, and the same foolishness. I can see your feelings run deep for this little motherless fawn. I know you can't help yourself. But death—that's natural as birth, Carrot, or eating or standing still and watching the wind shake the acorns off the trees. They can't all make it, all the fawns, all the does, or the woods would be overrun, the deer would strip every last leaf off every last tree. What I'm saying is, it's a kind of foolishness to want every last fawn to survive just because they look at you with their big, scared eyes. It's just not logical, Care. You have to let it go. You have to—"

He stopped talking and looked at her for a long, silent minute. Then he stood up, went over to the fawn, scooped it up, and carried it home to Babe.

Now Carrot turned away from her mother and looked back out the window. She saw her father, kneeling in the tomato plants, digging with a blue spade. Hot tears spilled down her cheeks.

She felt her mother's touch on her shoulder. "I—please don't be angry, Carrie. I—I love you."

"I love you, too," Carrot murmured. But it was her father out in the garden she was talking to.

11

"'It was a very dubious-looking, nay, a very dark and dismal night, bitingly cold and cheerless. I knew no one in the place. With anxious grapnels—'" Carrot stopped reading and looked to the notes at the bottom of the page. "Grapnels: hands."

"Hands," she said to Babe. "Grapnels are hands."

Babe made no pretense of listening to *Moby-Dick*. He had Henny Penny upside down between his knees and was carefully greasing the opening where her eggs came out. Gram had determined that Henny Penny was sluggish because, as she put it, "There's a traffic jam in her oviduct." Two or three eggs were stuck up inside her, and if they couldn't drop Henny Penny would probably die. Babe sat holding her under the big metal lamp that they had used on the chicks when they first hatched. Warmth was supposed to ease the passage of the eggs.

"Let your eggs come down, let your eggs come down, let your eggs come down, let—" Babe chanted, as if Henny Penny only needed to be coaxed into dropping her eggs.

"There's so many hard words in this book. I'm never going to get through it," Carrot said, tossing it on top of a bale. "'Anxious grapnels,' 'judiciously buttered,' 'Leviathan.' This guy must have been writing with a big, fat dictionary beside him." She snorted. "He must have kept one anxious grapnel on the dictionary at all times." She watched Babe's gentle stroking. "How's she doing?"

Babe sighed. "You see, Carrot, I can feel 'em. I can feel 'em but I can't get at 'em. I gotta bring her in the house."

"Inside?" Carrot asked. "Where?"

"Kitchen," Babe said, turning Henny Penny right side up and stroking her like a lapdog.

"You can't," Carrot said. "There's going to be all those women flapping around. That would only upset her."

"Oh." Babe considered this. "I'll put her in the bathtub."

"Right," Carrot said.

"Hey, guys—" Beaut stuck her head in the chicken coop, bringing in the fruity smell of green apples. "They're waiting for you up at the house." She smiled at Carrot. "Your hair looks darling."

Carrot rolled her eyes and tried not to picture Little Orphan Annie, which is exactly how she looked with her hair in about two hundred sausages her mother had crimped all over her head.

She held Henny Penny while Babe locked the fence and shoved the cinder block back in place. When they got to the house Babe disappeared upstairs with Henny Penny, and her mother seized Carrot by the hand. "There are so many people here," she said, putting her hands to her cheeks. "I never imagined they would all come."

Her mother's nervousness made Carrot want to run back to the chicken coop. She looked across the kitchen counter at the long room full of chattering women. She was surprised to see Mrs. Smoznak dressed in vivid orange. She had thought they would all be old women Gram's age. She was even more surprised to see Gram wearing a dress—it was brown wool, too heavy for this warm June night, but it was the first time Carrot had ever seen Gram in anything but blue jeans. Then she remembered. Gram had worn it once before, at the funeral.

Gram stood in front of the moose head so that the antlers seemed to rise up out of her own head. "Ladies," she said sharply, then waited for them to quiet down. "If you don't already know, this is my daughter-in-law, Susan, and my two granddaughters, Arbuta and Carrie. That's my end of it, now why don't you just go around the room with your names."

Carrot liked Gram's way of handling things—not fussy, just sensible. Most of the ladies were neighbors of Gram's but Beaut had invited Lisanne, her employer, who stood up and passed out coupons to everyone for 10 percent off all lingerie. Beaut had also asked the mother of her new boyfriend, Andy. Mrs. Stencil was a tiny lady in a green pantsuit. She reminded Carrot of an elf. She stood up and said in a whispery little voice, "What a treat it is to be with this delightful family of this delightful girl." And she put her hand on Beaut's shoulder.

"How very delightful," Carrot muttered under her breath, wondering how she was going to make it through this whole, long evening.

When it was Mrs. Smoznak's turn she said she was pleased to be there because it gave her an opportunity to see one of her most interesting students. Carrot felt herself blush. *Interesting* was the word her mother used when she didn't want to say something was ugly or awful or boring. Mrs. Smoznak added, "I'm also here because I *love* color. Of course, you'd never know it," she said, smoothing her hands over her neon orange dress. She threw back her head and laughed and so did everyone else.

Then her mother went into her spiel. "Winter, spring, summer, fall—who's the fairest one of all?" she said, clasping her hands under her chin and smiling around the room at everyone. Carrot had to admit her mother did come to life when she talked about makeup. Even though Carrot hated her sausage curls she was glad to see her mother acting like a real person.

Gram was the first guinea pig, and Carrot tried not to laugh when her mother took Gram by the hand and led her to the middle of the living room. She pointed at the green kitchen stool. "Now just hop up there and we'll have a look at you," she said brightly, as if she were a doctor about to examine a six-year-old.

Gram had talked Carrot into doing this, but Carrot could see Gram wasn't the least bit happy to be doing it, either. She scowled and plunked herself down on the stool without a word.

"Now, ladies, perhaps you have never thought much about color, but I promise you that color has more impact than you ever imagined!" Her mother reached behind Gram into a tumble of colored chiffon scarves and pulled out a bright red one to drape around Gram's neck.

"Look!" she said, stepping back and holding out her hand, "just look at the difference."

Everyone went, "Oooooh."

She whipped off the scarf, revealing Gram's dark brown dress. "From this plain and drab older woman to this"— she replaced the red scarf—"bright and radiant sophisticate."

Gram didn't exactly look bright and radiant. She sat there glumly like someone on trial. But it didn't matter. Carrot's mother was getting her old rhythm back. "It's like magic, isn't it," she said brightly. "But of course it isn't magic. It's only a matter of finding the colors of your lifetime—the colors of your season." She put her hands on Gram's shoulders. "Clara here is a winter. As you can see she has a winter's fair skin, gray-blue eyes, and silver-gray hair." She leaned down close to Gram, studying her pale, wrinkled face. "Do you have any makeup on, Clara?"

Gram snorted.

"Fine, fine," she said, as though Gram had answered. "Now we'll show you an even more dramatic transformation." For the next twenty minutes she dabbed and brushed and painted Gram's face, all the while talking about the colors a winter should wear. "Icy blue," she said, painting blue crescents on Gram's droopy eyelids, "will make the winter woman sparkle."

Babe had come downstairs and he and Carrot stood alone in the corner of the room, watching in amazement as Gram's eyes, cheeks, and lips took on a kaleidoscope of colors.

"Yuck," Babe said, putting his hand over his eyes.

"Shhhh." Carrot jabbed him with her elbow and looked

around to see if anyone had heard. Mrs. Smoznak caught her eye and grinned. Carrot frowned, wondering again about the word interesting. She knew it didn't mean sweet and good-natured like Beaut. "Pass out the cookies," she whispered to Babe. If he was busy he would be less likely to say something terrible about Gram's face.

Babe went to the end of the room where the kitchen was and picked up the plate of shortbread Gram had baked that afternoon. He stuffed one of the thick yellow triangles in his mouth and started for the living room.

"Babe," Carrot hissed, suddenly remembering that she had last seen Babe rubbing Henny Penny's egg hole with Vaseline. "Did you wash your hands?"

Babe shook his head, the shortbread caught between his teeth.

"Jeez, Babe." She pointed at the sink and then started forward with the cookie tray. Again she caught Mrs. Smoznak grinning at her. Maybe interesting just means sort of goofy she thought, bending low with the cookie tray so she wouldn't block anyone's view of her mother and Gram.

When Gram was finished everyone clapped and made appreciative noises and told Gram how wonderful she looked and how she should always wear cherry red. Gram came back in the kitchen and stood between Carrot and Babe. "Feel like a damn Christmas tree," she grumbled. Babe stared at her but Carrot looked at the floor. With her blue and pink eyes and bright red cheeks Gram reminded Carrot of the clown on the cornflakes box, except on Gram it wasn't funny.

Her mother did Beaut next and nothing went wrong.

Beaut just sat there smiling and looking beautiful while her mother draped her in "spring colors" and put peachy stuff on her face and turquoise powder on her eyes. Beaut had sat for so many of her mother's demos that she even filled in words as her mother went along. "Spring's colors are the hardest to find," her mother said. "They must be—"

"Clear, never muted," Beaut said.

"And not too dark," her mother added, flinging a violet cape around Beaut's shoulders.

With her golden tan and her tumble of blond hair, Beaut would have looked good in a feed sack, but with makeup on she looked like a movie star—a twenty-five-year-old movie star. She was a wonderful advertisement for her mother's products.

"I'd buy the whole suitcase full of makeup if I could look like that," Carrot heard someone say. When Beaut was finished all the women wanted to check her eyes, touch her hair, just inspect her at close range. They better not try that with me, Carrot thought. She dreaded sitting up there on the stool in front of everyone with her sausage head.

"And now—" her mother said, brightly. Carrot looked over at Babe and whispered the words at the same time her mother said them—"my crimson bonnet." She made a face at Babe and then went into the living room and perched on the stool.

"A perfect autumn," her mother said, beaming at Carrot. "You see the ivory skin with its golden undertones." She lifted Carrot's arm and held it, palm out, for inspection. "And of course the hair." Carrot sensed a tinge of disappointment in her voice. They both knew there should have been more hair. She was pointing out the gold flecks in

97

Carrot's irises when everyone in the room started to laugh. Carrot looked to her left and there was Henny Penny, red and fat, at the foot of the stairs. She was sitting the way she did when she was going to lay an egg, and in a moment she squawked and stood up and sure enough, she had left a perfect brown egg on the hallway runner.

"Oh, my," Carrot's mother said, putting her hand over her heart. "Oh, Babe, would you mind—"

But Babe, arms outstretched, was hovering over Henny Penny who had now moved into the living room and was squawking and flapping violently. He held up a hand. "Quiet, quiet, quiet. Everyone quiet. She's gonna lay another egg."

The women giggled and drew back their shoes as Henny Penny strutted by. "A pet chicken," someone said. "Freshest eggs in town—floor to the table." This was followed by peals of laughter.

In another minute Henny Penny settled under the table and there was a nervous silence while everyone waited to see what would happen next.

"How can she lay another one?" someone whispered. "Chickens don't do that."

But she did. With a loud cackle Henny Penny stood up and at her feet was another little brown egg.

All the women started applauding and exclaiming about Henny Penny, the wonder chicken.

Now Carrot's mother walked over to Henny Penny with her hands on her hips and said, as if she were speaking to a naughty child, "You've got to go back to the chicken coop for that sort of thing. I simply can't carry on with chickens laying eggs all over the place." She looked at Babe and then decided instead to appeal to Carrot. "Sweetheart, would you—"

"No!" Babe spread his arms over Henny Penny like a canopy. "You see, she isn't done. There's another one, I know there's another one." He started rocking back and forth, hitting his head with his hands.

Carrot came over and squeezed his arm. "It's okay," she whispered, wishing she and Babe were back in the coop.

But Gram wasn't the least embarrassed. "Don't you stew, Babe," she said, putting her arms around him. "Henny Penny is going to be fine. Nobody's going to throw her out. We'll just take a little coffee break and give Henny Penny some space to finish her business. You ladies don't mind, do you?"

"Clara, really," Carrot's mother said, wringing a plum scarf between her hands. "My demonstration—"

But everyone said, "No, that's okay. We can eat cookies and be entertained at the same time." They thought Henny Penny was a great show.

Beaut passed the cookies again and Carrot took around coffee, and everyone started eating and talking and laughing all at once. Mrs. Smoznak held up her empty cup and beamed at Carrot. "Having a good summer, Carrot?"

Carrot poured her coffee and nodded.

"And are you enjoying *Moby-Dick*?"

"Oh, yeah," Carrot said, hurrying on to the next lady.

"How far are you?"

Carrot poured for Mrs. Stencil and asked her if she would like some cream, pretending that she hadn't heard the question.

After a half hour or so Babe held up his hand. "Please

everyone, please everyone, shut up." A hush fell over the women as they all turned to look at Henny Penny under the table. She jerked her head from side to side, accusing everyone with her bright black eyes. She stood up. She sat down. She fluffed her feathers. She got up and walked in a nervous little circle, cackling loudly. Finally she sat down in earnest for a full three minutes, and when she stood up there was a third brown egg.

Now everyone cheered. Henny Penny was an incredible chicken. Three eggs in one night. Babe picked her up and walked around the room, and the women all got out of their seats to make a fuss over her.

"Babe, now could you remove her to the chicken coop?" Carrot's mom pointed to the back door. She had been sitting in silence off to one side, folding scarves and moving around her little jars of makeup while the other women chatted and sipped their coffee.

Gram nodded at Babe, and Carrot ran out the back door after him before her mother could stop her.

It was dark outside and the unfamiliar autos gleamed in the moonlight. Carrot ran her hands over a white, rounded fender as she passed it on the way to the coop.

She caught up with Babe. "She's okay now, isn't she?"

"Good old Penny's okey-dokey," Babe said, nuzzling his big head down against Henny Penny's neck. "A good old worker and a good old pal," he sang, "sixteen miles on the Erie Canal." His deep, booming voice seemed to lift over the housetop and fill the night, all the way to the woods.

"Low bridge, everybody down," Carrot sang, spreading her arms to the whole star-bright universe. Henny Penny wasn't going to die. Carrot didn't have to sit in front of twenty ladies with gooey glop all over her face. She and Babe had the whole warm summer stretching in front of them before she had to go back to school. She breathed in the sweet June air, watching Babe round the chicken coop ahead of her.

Then she heard him.

"No!" he yelled. "No, no, no, no!"

Carrot ran around the coop and found him squatting before the open gate.

"The chickens," he said, looking up at her. "The chickens are gone."

12

Of course it had been the Horning boys. Gram knew it right away. "Those devils," she said. "They're the only ones on God's green earth mean enough to do this. Break in and steal every one of Babe's chickens. It's not enough to torment him every time they see him. They have to destroy his entire business."

Carrot and Gram were sitting at the kitchen table drinking coffee the morning after the Rainbow party. Plates of cookies and half-empty cups were scattered around the room. Only her mother's makeup and scarf collection had been neatly put away and stored in two black suitcases behind the sofa.

"Break his heart," Gram added, and they both turned to look at Babe who had pulled the stool against the living room wall and was sitting there with his back to them, his head to the wall.

"Why?" Gram asked, pressing her thumb between her eyebrows and closing her eyes. "If they're going to go on a rampage, why don't they go after me? I'm the one reported them for shining. Not Babe. Babe has never hurt a soul. He's the most harmless, the most gentle person in this whole town." She picked up her cup and put it back down without drinking. "Maybe that's why. They just can't stand his goodness." She stared over the counter and out the kitchen window without saying a word. Then she looked back at Carrot. "It's like tying a tin can to a kitten's tail. He doesn't understand. How could he? I don't understand myself."

But Carrot understood. She had been up almost all night thinking about what had happened. Mr. Eggs was out of business and it was all her fault. The Horning boys had figured out who had flattened their tires and stolen their clothes after they had seen Carrot and Babe on the road. But Babe had nothing to do with it. He had pleaded with her not to mess with Bert and Dudley. She had been so anxious for revenge, so certain she knew better than Babe. Looking at Babe in the corner of the room she hung her head. How would she ever make it up to him? She stared into the creamy tan circle of her cup, wondering how to tell Gram. Finally she took a deep breath. "Gram," she said softly.

Just then Beaut and her mother came down the stairs, full of chatter about the night before. "She's a sweet little thing," Susan said, "but green—well, it's just really not her color."

"Mom," Beaut wailed, "I hope you didn't—"

"Of course not, of course not," she said, giggling at Beaut's forlorn expression. "I told her, but I told her very delicately that—oh, good morning everyone." She stopped at the bottom of the stairs and beamed at Carrot and

Gram, waving a stack of index cards over her head. "I sold seven bottles of Silky Skin, three Lids'N'Lashes, four lipsticks, and I have—umm—" She flipped through the cards. "I have four appointments to do Rainbow makeovers. I would say that last night was a resounding success in spite of—ah—a few interruptions."

"Not exactly a resounding success." Gram got up and dumped her coffee in the sink.

Her mother's smile faded as she looked from Carrot to Gram and then over to Babe, his face still pressed to the wall. She brought her fist up to her mouth in that quick gesture of panic that was so familiar to Carrot. It was Beaut who spoke first.

"What happened?"

"Somebody broke into the coop and stole Babe's chickens last night."

"All of them?" Beaut's eyes opened in amazement.

"All but the chicks," Gram said. "And Jupiter. And of course we had Henny Penny in here."

Susan sank into the chair, her hands on either side of her face. "Who?" she asked. "Why?"

Before Gram could answer Carrot took a deep breath and said, "It was Dudley and Bert Horning and they did it because I flattened all the tires on their truck and because I stole their clothes when they were swimming at the gravel pit. Babe had nothing to do with it. It was all my idea."

There was a stillness in the room as Gram, Beaut, and her mother stared at her. Through the window Carrot could see the garden sprinklers arcing silver in the morning sunlight. She wished she were out in the garden pulling weeds or picking green tomato worms off the plants. Anywhere else, even in her English class. "And I know it doesn't help but I'm sorry," she added, looking back down at her cold toast.

"Sorry?" her mother shrieked, stabbing the air with her finger. "That's a criminal offense. Stealing. Vandalism. Carissa Turvy, when are you going to rein in that temper of yours? You get mad at me—you cut your hair. You get mad at these two boys and you risk life and limb to get revenge." Now she stood up and shook her finger in Carrot's face. "Trouble follows trouble and that's what you are with a capital *T*. Those boys could have run you over with that big old truck. They could have broken every bone in your body. You're lucky, that's what you are. You're lucky it was only a bunch of silly chickens."

"Oh, shut up, Susan," Gram said, starting to pile up the dirty plates. "It's all spilled milk now."

In the days that followed Carrot spent every morning in the garden. She got up, got a cup of coffee from Gram, and went straight outside in time to see the sun, pale as water, poke its face up above the woods behind her. In June there was always weeding to be done, always composting, always spraying soapy water for bugs. It felt good to sit there in the damp grass beside the rows, sipping coffee, surveying their work. She could see the growth from one day to the next; the green beans grew fatter, the tomatoes pinker, the zucchini flowered overnight. And all around the garden and beyond the cornfield, on up the hill to the woods, the daisies were in bloom, brightening the grass like summer snow. When she sat like this or when she went down on all fours, pulling weeds, clawing up the packed soil with her little rake, hoeing, sweating in the morning sun, she felt okay. The sorrow over what she had done to Babe disappeared. The deeper, sucking emptiness was better, too. Sometimes, reaching into the cool greenness of the beans, she would pause and sit back on her heels, thinking about Ruby Dodd, about the killing part. But mostly she tried not to think.

On Sunday mornings, when Gram took Babe to Sunday school, Carrot took care of the chicks. Babe had been going to Sunday school for years, helping Mrs. Strobel by leading the singing and helping the little kids color Bible stories. To him it was as much of a job as selling produce or tending the chicks. Not being holy, as she said, Gram spent the hour drinking coffee and reading the *Peelee Daily* at Lindsay's Drugstore.

Now standing in the chicken yard gave Carrot a hollow feeling in her stomach. Henny Penny and the dozen chicks came running when she started scattering scraps from the red bowl. But it was nothing like the wild scramble of all the hens and all the chicks squawking, and dusting and pecking each other to be the first. It seemed like a feeble nursery school group now. Even Jupiter didn't bother with them. He just stood on an upturned pail and looked off toward the woods as if he were bored.

After she dumped the bowl Carrot picked up Henny Penny and carried her down the drive to the produce stand. It was a white wooden counter with a front and sides that Babe and her father had built years ago, and it had a big flat roof that extended back about ten feet where it was attached to long posts. The roof gave them shade and enough room to store all the vegetables for the day. She and Babe had painted a green sign across the front of the counter that said TURVY'S PRODUCE. And then they had painted a tomato, an ear of corn, a beet, and a green bean in the corners of the sign. It was all kind of lopsided but it was colorful.

She sat down behind the counter in an aluminum folding chair and put Henny Penny on her lap. "At least they didn't get *you*," she said, stroking her back. "Wormy slimebags." Henny Penny turned her head and stared at Carrot out of her accusing little black eyes. Carrot sighed. "I'm the wormy slimebag. It's my fault you don't have any sisters left, that you don't have anyone to sit around and lay eggs with. Henny Penny, nobody else in the whole world has a temper like mine. I'm just plain mean. Mean as the Horning boys. I've ruined your life, I've ruined Babe's life, I've ruined—"

A car pulled up and Carrot tensed. She hated waiting on customers. Babe was much better at talking to people than she was. A lady and a man got out dressed up like they were on their way back from church. "How're your tomatoes?" the man asked.

Carrot pointed at the baskets on the counter. She didn't go into great raving descriptions or try to push things on people. If they liked what they saw, they bought. If they didn't, they didn't buy.

"Fine," the woman said, opening her purse. "We'll take two pounds." Then she reached over and plucked a green bean out of a basket and snapped it. "Nice and fresh," she said to Carrot. "Better give us a pound of those, too. And what about eggs?" She looked down at Henny Penny as if she expected her to answer.

Carrot shook her head.

Her husband leaned over the counter. "Mr. Eggs," he said, as if Carrot had not understood.

"He's out of business," she said, dumping the green beans into a paper bag.

"Oh, well, in that case," the wife said, "we don't want anything. We really just wanted the eggs. Somebody told us about the eggs."

They walked back to their car leaving Carrot holding a bag of tomatoes and a bag of green beans. "Crazy," she said to Henny Penny, picking her up again and sinking back into the chair. People were always surprising her. Once a truck driver stopped and offered them nine dollars if they would cook a vegetable stew like his mother used to make. He left the recipe with them, and she and Babe cooked the stew that night and he picked it up the next day. He was so happy she felt a little sorry for him—that he was too stupid to cook a bunch of vegetables together for himself.

Another car stopped and Carrot looked up. It was Babe and Gram. Gram let Babe out then leaned toward the open window. "How's—" She stopped to sneeze. "Stupid time of year to catch a cold," she grumbled. "How's business?"

Carrot shook her head. "Everyone's at church."

"Be patient," Gram said, sneezing again. She blew her nose and then waved and started down the drive.

"I can't be patient," Carrot yelled at Babe. She thumped the counter. "I want to sell everything now. I want to sell all our tomatoes, all our green beans, all our peas, all our carrots right this minute. I want a hundred people to come immediately and spend ten dollars each, and I want to make a thousand dollars *right now*. And then I want to run through the sprinkler in my shorts and then I want to ride my bike to the Dairy Delite and get a Velvet Thundercloud." She threw a tomato in the air and caught it. "And then I want to hike up to the top of Weenie Hill."

Babe laughed. "Go on, Carrot," he said. "Go run in the sprinkler. I'll stay here. You see, I'm more patient." He picked up Henny Penny and started petting her.

Carrot sat down beside him. "I hate it when you're so nice, Babe. Why are you so nice?" She leaned over and thumped him on his thick shoulder. "Are you trying to make me feel guilty?"

"Naa-aw," he said, looking embarrassed. "I'm not *so* nice. I'm just—I'm just usual nice."

"But you *are*, Babe. You're the nicest person I know." Carrot looked at Babe in his funny red bow tie, rubbing his fat cheek against Henny Penny's head, and she realized it was true. He was nicer than Beaut, nicer than Gram, in a way even nicer than her father, because he never lost his temper and yelled at her, not even the night of the chickens. And he always had a smile for her no matter how terrible she was.

She got up and hugged him around the neck. "I'm so sorry I hurt you, Babe. That I ruined Mr. Eggs."

He squeezed her hand. "It's okay, Carrot. I told you a hundred times, it's okay. Hey—you wanna hear what I learned at Sunday school?" Without waiting for an answer he started singing in his deep booming voice. "'Ezekiel saw the wheel way up in the middle of the air, Ezekiel saw the wheel way up in the middle of the air, a wheel in a wheel in a wheel in a wheel, way up in the middle of the air.'"

Carrot laughed. "Pretty weird song."

But Babe just kept on singing, "'Way up in the middle of the air—'"

He sang it over and over, and Carrot pictured a big shiny wheel with silver spokes spinning around in the blue sky. Except for some reason she pictured it spinning over Ruby Dodd's lavender house, sort of like a flying saucer. She wondered if Ruby Dodd had come from another planet. "Hey, Babe—"

He stopped singing.

"Does Ruby Dodd have any children?"

He shook his head. "Just the goat. That old goat ate a whole carton of my eggs one time. And the carton too."

"Well, does she have a—like a husband or anything?"

"Husband? I don't know. Want me to look next time, Carrot?"

She shook her head. "What else can she do besides tell fortunes?"

Babe scratched the top of his head with his index finger. "She can drive a truck. She can bake cookies with those sprinkle things."

Carrot wanted to know if Ruby Dodd could pluck stars out of the night or if she turned people into turnips. Most of all she wanted to know about the killing part. What did it mean? It made her shiver every time she thought about it. It was all tangled up with thoughts of her father dying and the cruelty of the Horning boys. What did Ruby Dodd have to do with any of that? But she knew things. She knew about Carrot's bucket of tears. And she knew—Carrot had never told anyone—about hiding away from the world. Sometimes Carrot wanted to run from Gram's farm, away from everyone she knew, to another country or another world, someplace dark and hidden like a cave or underneath the earth where her father had gone. Carrot got down off her chair and curled up under the counter where she could think. Gram always said Carrot reminded her of a chipmunk because she liked to curl up in dark corners.

Above her she could hear Babe start to sing again, "'A wheel in a wheel in a wheel in a wheel—'" But then there was another voice and he stopped.

"Hi, Dan," Babe said. He set Henny Penny down, so Carrot reached out and pulled her under the counter. "Cluck, cluck, cluck," she said softly, grinning at the fat chicken.

"We got green peppers and lotsa more tomatoes back here in the shade. You wanna come back? People like to pick it out their selves. Here's the bag."

In a second Carrot saw a pair of long wiry legs walk past the counter and red shorts bending over the tomatoes. She squinched herself tighter under the counter. When he turned she saw who it was—the Dan from her English class—Dan Durbin. She held her breath, hoping he wouldn't look her way. If only she could crawl out and hide in the bushes till he left.

"This looks good," he said to Babe. "My mom needs a bunch for a barbecue this afternoon." He kept stuffing tomatoes in the bag, not checking them for bruises or spots. "Are you going to help us with the wood this fall? Mom said to be sure and ask you."

"Yup," Babe said. "Pretty soon. After the garden. Me

and Carrot have to finish the spinach and put in some more peas. After that then."

Dan looked up. "You and who?"

Carrot sucked in her breath and wished she would turn invisible.

"Her," Babe said, pointing under the counter. "Carrot."

Dan's gaze followed Babe's finger and he looked directly into Carrot's eyes. A big grin spread over his face and he set the bag on the ground and came over and squatted, turning his head sideways to look at her. "It looks like you're having a great summer."

Carrot smiled feebly.

He nodded at Henny Penny. "Nice chicken."

"That's Henny Penny," Babe offered.

Dan looked up at Babe. "Do you ever let them out of there?"

"Sure," Babe said.

"C'mon, Carrot," Dan said. Like he was coaxing a puppy from under the bed.

Carrot let go of Henny Penny and crawled out. "I was resting," she said crabbily.

Dan nodded. "I always like to curl up with a big chicken when I'm tired."

She could feel her cheeks burning. "So did you want those tomatoes or what?" she asked, kicking at an imaginary stone.

"You live here with Babe and the old woman?"

"Gram," she snapped.

"I thought you had vanished into thin air. Don't you ever go into town? Do you ever go to the Cube for a sandwich or to the gravel pit?"

"Nope," she said. "Here's your tomatoes. Two bucks."

He handed her the money and dropped the plastic bag over his handlebars. "I work at the Dairy Delite. Come and see me sometime—I'll fix you a Velvet Thundercloud. Carissa," he added. Then he grinned and pedaled away.

"Carrot," she grumbled. "My name is Carrot." But he was already gone.

13

*C*arrot opened her eyes and saw the outline of Beaut in the moonlight leaning over her.

"Carrot," she whispered. "Hey, are you okay? Was it a nightmare?"

Carrot groaned and scootched across the bed into Beaut's arms. For a second she didn't say anything. She just let herself breathe in Beaut's sweet-apple warmth, trying to forget the dream. She had dreamed about her father before, lots of times, about walking in the woods with him, even about him falling from the roof and her not being able to catch him.

Finally she took a deep breath. "It was awful," she said to Beaut. "There was a huge gun, like a cannon, and it was up high, on a cliff overlooking Peelee. Way higher than Weenie Hill. And we were packed inside the barrel like bullets and then there was this huge bang and we got shot out way up into the sky." She stopped, feeling herself flying through the air again, and it made her stomach lurch. "There was blood," she said. "We were bleeding from all over our bodies. And every part of me hurt, even my pinkie fingers—" She lifted her hands and looked at them in the dark, still expecting to feel pain. "We were all screaming because we were going to fall a hundred miles to the ground."

"Was it Daddy?" Beaut asked.

Carrot nodded. "And me, and it was Babe and . . . somebody else." She closed her eyes for a second and saw him. Tall, skinny, dark haired, with ears that stuck out. "It was a boy from my English class. Dan. I—I don't even know him. It was so creepy, Beaut."

Beaut lay down beside Carrot and put her arms around her. "I know. I hate it when I dream of Daddy."

"What do you dream?"

Beaut sighed. "I don't know. I make myself forget."

"Like how?"

"As soon as I wake up I redesign everything. I make it all bright and happy. I picture me riding Daddy's shoulders going down Concord to the Thanksgiving parade like we used to," she said, twisting Carrot's hair around her finger. "You were just a baby, I think."

"What else?" Carrot asked, starting to relax.

"Oh, I think about Sunday nights when you and Daddy would be coming back from Gram's and I would stand by the window and watch for him, and he would go, 'Shave and a haircut—two bits,' with the horn all the way down the street."

"Yeah," Carrot said. "Every time."

"And when he got inside he would pick me up and twirl me around—"

Carrot's eyes flew open. "Beaut—I just remembered

another part. There was a big wheel, a big silver wheel spinning in the sky above us. And there was a person— Ruby Dodd—sitting on that wheel and just watching. Not trying to help us. Just watching."

"Go back to sleep," Beaut said, yawning. "It's just a silly dream."

In the morning neither of them mentioned Carrot's dream. Beaut was rushing around getting ready for work and Carrot sat on the edge of the bed waiting for her to leave so she could get dressed without getting in her way.

"Would you pick out some decent tomatoes?" Beaut asked. She was standing in front of the mirror, putting lipstick on and feeling around with her right foot for her shoe. "Andy's going to stop by this afternoon for some tomatoes and some—I don't know—squash or something. Just make sure it's decent, would you?"

"It's all decent," Carrot said, kicking the shoe over to her. "We wouldn't sell it if it wasn't."

"God, I hope we're not as busy as we were yesterday. Andy's picking me up at five-thirty to go to the Howlett County Fair. And we've got this fifty-off sale on bras and girdles. I never saw so much blubber as I did yesterday."

Carrot snorted. Then she thought of Dan Durbin. It was the word *blubber*. She wondered again why he had been in her dream. He was such an embarrassing jerk. She hoped he never showed up at the produce stand again. And he'd better stay out of her dreams.

"Ta-ta." Beaut waved her fingers and started out the door.

"Hey, Beaut?"

She paused and looked at Carrot.

"Does he ever kiss you?"

Beaut rolled her eyes and went out the door.

Beaut's boyfriend, Andy, showed up at the produce stand around noon. Babe was eating a sandwich and Carrot was trying to finish chapter 13 of *Moby-Dick*. She had skipped the chapters between two and twelve where the guy, Ishmael, walked around New Bedford musing. He was always musing about fate and humanity and death and other dull stuff. But now Ishmael and Queequeg were on the ship to Nantucket going through stormy seas. "Listen to this part," she said.

"Queequeg, stripped to the waist, darted from the side with a long, living arc of a leap. For three minutes or more he was seen swimming like a dog, throwing his long arms straight out before him, and by turns revealing his brawny shoulders through the freezing foam. I looked at the grand and glorious fellow, but saw no one to be saved. The greenhorn had gone down. Shooting himself perpendicularly from the water, Queequeg now took an instant's glance around him, and seeming to see just how matters were, dived down and disappeared. A few minutes more, and he rose again, one arm still striking out, and with the other dragging a lifeless form. The boat soon picked them up. The poor bumpkin was restored."

She shut the book. "Queequeg saved his life."

Babe nodded. "That's a funny name. I had a caterpillar named Sweepea."

"See, Babe, the bumpkin was making fun of him because he was big and brown and had tattoos on his face. But

Queequeg showed that he was a better person." She sighed. "I think that's what it means." This was such a hard book, with more horrible words like "anxious grapnels" than she had ever read before. And there weren't many good parts. She wondered if it was worth all this trouble to change her grade.

A little blue convertible drove up, and Babe put his sandwich down and pulled up the neck of his T-shirt to wipe his mouth. Carrot sat back with her book. When she saw that it was Andy she looked up.

"Hi, there." He put his hands on the counter and leaned toward Carrot. Andy was one of the rich kids in town. He owned his own car and he dressed like a character in a Spiegel catalogue, in striped shirts and matching vests, and his hair was perfect. Even today, when it was ninety out, his brown hair was parted just so and plastered back on both sides. He reminded Carrot of a Ken doll. "I'll bet you have some tomatoes for me, don't you?"

"Right beside you." She pointed.

"I—uh—I kind of wanted some special ones."

"Give him some special ones, Babe." She knew if Beaut were waiting on him she would be flinging herself all over the place looking for the perfect tomatoes. She could tell he was one of those people who expected everyone to knock themselves out for him. She turned another page.

Babe picked up a carton of tomatoes and started emptying it into a paper bag. "One or two?"

"I—ah—beg your pardon?" He looked at Babe for the first time. "Oh—ah—that would be two pounds, Mr.—ummmm. . . ." His voice trailed off and he turned around and looked at his car. "Great day for a convertible. Wind in your hair. Your sister loves this car," he said to Carrot.

Carrot kept her eyes on the book. She was annoyed that Andy was ignoring Babe. He wouldn't even look at him.

"Well, so long." He rapped his fingertips on the counter. "Should I pay you or—umm—should I pay him?"

Carrot glared at him. "Pay him."

He pulled away, snapping gravel back against the side of the stand.

"That's Beaut's boyfriend," Babe said, watching the car till it was out of sight. "He drives a pretty car."

Carrot snorted. "That's the nicest thing about him." She poured some lemonade for Babe and some for herself. Then she went back to her chair in the shade. She watched Babe choose a crayon from a tin can at his feet. He picked a red, held it up to a tomato, shook his head and picked an orangish red that matched. He was coloring vegetable place mats for the Sunday school class.

"Don't people get on your nerves, Babe?"

He shook his head and reached for a green crayon.

"Do you like everyone?"

"Nope, I don't like Dudley and I don't like Bert. I can't stand Dudley and Bert. They make me wanna puke."

"But you like everyone else?"

Babe didn't answer right away. She watched him concentrate on drawing long skinny green beans all around the border of his place mat. "One time Jesse told me to don't worry about loving everyone. Just worry about loving yourself."

Her father had told her, too. How could you love yourself, she wondered, when you were always messing up, always losing your temper, or else worrying about messing up and losing your temper? "Well, do you?" she asked.

But before he answered Dan Durbin pulled up on his bike. "Howdy." He was wearing a Detroit Tigers cap and he lifted it like it was a cowboy hat. He swung off his bike and walked to the counter and watched Babe coloring. "That green bean is too skinny."

Babe put down his crayon and studied the green bean.

"I came to get some green beans but if they're that feeble, I don't know. I'll show you what I want. Give me that crayon."

Babe shook his head. "I'll fix it myself."

"I don't know, Babe. I hope you're a better farmer than you are an artist." He watched as Babe colored over every green bean on his place mat. "Okay." He slapped his hand on the counter. "Give me some green beans just like that."

Babe put down the crayon and moved toward the green beans.

"Hold on," Dan said, taking his hat off and pointing it at Babe. "Can't that girl do anything? The one you keep under the counter?"

Babe laughed and Carrot groaned.

"She's not under the counter. She's right there." Babe pointed.

Of course he knew she was there. He just had to try and embarrass her again. She put down her book and came to the counter. "How many did you want?" she asked, eyeing him coolly.

"Hi, Carrot." He grinned like he was making fun of her.

"A pound?" she asked. "Two pounds?"

120

"Two pounds of the fattest green beans you have. And a dozen eggs."

"We no longer have eggs," she said crisply.

"Somebody stole all my layers," Babe added. "All but Henny Penny."

"No kidding," Dan said, and his voice lost its mocking tone. "Who did it?"

Carrot shut her mouth and crossed her arms over her chest. But of course Babe answered. He'd tell anyone anything.

"Bert and Dudley," he said. "Because Carrot gave them four flat tires and stole their clothes."

Dan looked at Carrot and whistled, which made his Adam's apple stick out in his neck. "I guess you *are* a wild woman." He picked up the green crayon and tapped it against the counter. "Or else you're nuts."

Carrot stared back at him. "I'm not nuts."

"I guess those scumbags must have done something pretty bad to deserve that?

"They—"

"Babe," Carrot interrupted him, "why don't you weigh the beans?"

Even after Dan paid for the beans he was in no hurry to take off. "I've got another hour before I start work," he said, stretching out on the grass and watching them wait on customers, which made Carrot so nervous that she overcharged someone fifty cents on a bag of tomatoes. Finally he stood up. "Gotta shove off. Thanks for the lemonade." When he turned around to get his green beans off the counter a blue truck sped by.

"Ba-a-a-beee!"

Carrot groaned and Babe covered his face with his hands.

"Was that who I think it was?" Dan asked. They watched as the truck turned around and sped toward them. It stopped inches away from Dan's ten-speed.

"Hi, kiddies." Bert Horning hung his head out the window, his dirty-blond hair hanging in his eyes. "Whatcha selling?"

Nobody answered.

"Guess we'd better take a look, huh, Dudley?" He said something to his brother and they both got out of the truck laughing.

Carrot stepped over to Babe and took his hand.

Bert walked up to the counter, picked a tomato out of the display basket and bit into it. He grinned at Carrot, juice dripping down his chin. "Got any eggs for sale?"

"Yeah," said Dudley. "It'd be good to have some eggs scrambled up with these here tomatoes." He patted his bare stomach, which was thin and hard and shiny with sweat.

Carrot tightened her grip on Babe's hand and considered smashing a tomato into Dudley's ham-colored face.

"The chickens are all gone," Babe said, before Carrot could stop him.

Dan stepped closer to the counter. "In a way, it was kind of a blessing. Because we were going to destroy them anyhow." He shook his head. "With the disease and all."

Dudley's eye twitched. "Disease?"

"Oh, it's that blood disease that chickens get," Dan scratched his head, "called—"

Carrot came up beside him. "Anxious grapnels."

"Right." Dan looked at her and nodded. "Anxious grapnels. Makes them puff up, and pretty soon you can't even see their eyes."

"The two chickens that were left," Carrot sighed, "we had to kill them." She sensed Babe was about to say something and she stepped on his foot.

Bert looked at Dudley. "What for?"

"Well, you can't eat the eggs, that's for sure. And you sure don't want to eat the chickens, not with that stuff in their bloodstream. Yech." Dan made a face. "If you ever ate any chicken parts, even a drumstick, with anxious grapnels you might feel all right at first."

"Yeah," Carrot said, "just a little tired."

"Right." Dan nodded. "A little punk at first, then it starts working on your stomach. There was this guy I know whose stomach blew up like he was nine months pregnant. It's probably the trots that are the worst part of it."

"That and your tongue," Carrot said.

Bert set his half-eaten tomato on the counter. "This ain't any good," he said. "None of this stuff is." He turned and stalked to his truck.

"Crap," said Dudley, kicking the produce stand and then following his brother.

Carrot, her mouth hanging open, watched them shoot off down the road. She looked at Dan.

"Haaaaa!" he yelled, lifting his hand to her.

She high-fived him. Then they both collapsed on the grass in hysterics.

14

*W*hen Carrot got up in the morning the kitchen was dark. She put her hand on the coffee pot. Cold. So Gram was feeling no better. It made her uneasy, Gram being sick, even if it was just a summer cold like she said. She grabbed a banana and sank down into a chair at the table, wondering if she should take a pot of tea to Gram's bedroom. Gram never drank tea but it was what her mother made for Carrot and Beaut when they were sick. She chewed the banana and listened to the drip of the leaky faucet. A waste of water, she thought. These first days of August had been scorching and there hadn't been a drop of rain in three weeks. From down in the cellar she could hear the rhythmic clicking of the water pump that was keeping the garden from withering in the fierce sun. Already, at seven in the morning, she could smell the hot dust from outside the kitchen window, and with it the odor of scorched oatmeal cookies. She and Babe had been trying to help out but they got involved in a tick-tack-toe marathon and burned four dozen of them. Things just didn't go smoothly without Gram.

In the living room all the curtains had been drawn against the heat, and in the darkness the silhouette of the old moose head was bleaker than usual. Dead and not dead, she thought, shuddering. Sometimes when she was alone in the room she threw Gram's afghan over his head. Now the afghan was on the floor under a welter of colored squares of material. Carrot thought about putting away the pieces for Gram's crazy quilt until she was better. But she just sat there, scratching at a mosquito bite, waiting for Babe.

By the time Babe showed up her lethargy had passed. She watched him pour cornflakes in his bowl. "Let's hurry and get out there before it gets too hot," she said.

Babe shoveled down the cereal and filled up his bowl again. He shook his head. "I'm going to Ruby Dodd's."

Carrot's eyebrows shot up. "What for? You don't have any eggs."

"I'm diggin' her a new well."

"A new well? A well?" she said again, trying to think of a reason that Babe shouldn't dig a well for Ruby Dodd.

"An' we're gonna bring her some tomatoes, she ask me, and some beans an', uhh—Susan wrote it on a list." He pulled a piece of paper from his shirt pocket and handed it to Carrot. "An' you're coming, too," he said, pouring his third bowl of cereal.

"Me? No, I'm not," she said. "Somebody's got to work the garden. Somebody's got to run the stand. Who's going to run the stand?"

"Just for the morning," Babe said, wiping his mouth. "You pull the wagon, I carry the shovels. Susan said we should deliver the vegetables. It could be like Mr. Eggs, only tomatoes and cukes. She said I could be Mr. Cucumber until the chicks start layin'." He scratched his cheek. "Naw, I don't wanna be Mr. Cucumber. I just wanna be Mr. Eggs. Do you want me to be Mr. Cucumber, Carrot?" He laughed. "Hey, I could be Mr. Carrot and you could be Mrs. Carrot."

Carrot was too busy thinking about Ruby Dodd. "I'll just give her the vegetables and leave," she said. "I'm not going in her house or anything."

Babe patted her hand. "She won't hurt you, Carrot."

But it wasn't that, Carrot thought, pulling the rattly old red wagon full of vegetables down Bentley. It wasn't that she thought Ruby Dodd would hurt her. But what was it? Why did her heart race when she thought about Ruby Dodd in her purple house? She had a sudden image of Ruby Dodd whirling around in the sky on her silver wheel, watching every move Carrot made.

"'Tis the gift to be simple," Babe sang, "'tis the gift to be free, 'tis the gift to—"

"How can you be so cheerful?" Carrot complained. "It's about a hundred degrees out." Looking down the gray ribbon of road she could see heat waves dancing above it. The Queen Anne's lace by the side of the road was coated with dust and bent over like it was halfway to death. She squinted and everything—the green fields, the listless trees—became shimmering and distorted. Beside her Babe looked like a dancing ghost. She switched hands on the wagon and

126

plucked her sticky T-shirt away from her body. "I wish it would rain." She looked up at the fierce glare of the sun. "The garden's going to dry up," she said, frowning at Babe.

But he kept singing. The shovel blades bouncing on his big shoulders clanged against each other in noisy accompaniment, irritating Carrot even more. Following him down the rutted drive into Ruby Dodd's yard, she stopped scowling when she saw the goat standing in the doorway of the purple house.

"Hi, Tattoo," Babe said, dropping the shovels so that a puff of dust rose up in their faces.

Noticing the bare patches in the lawn Carrot realized that grass was probably Tattoo's main diet. She took a carrot from the wagon and went up on the porch. "Hey," she said, holding it out with one hand and ready to pat Tattoo's head with the other, if she'd let Carrot. The goat snatched the carrot from her fingers and gobbled it up so fast that her head did a little dance. Then she lowered her head and butted Carrot's shoulder. Carrot looked into the sober little face of the goat and laughed, forgetting how jittery she had been. "You want another one?" She went back to the wagon for two more carrots, and when she turned around the goat had stuck her head in the bag of tomatoes.

"Get yer head outa there or I'll chop it off!"

Carrot whirled around to see Ruby Dodd standing at the corner of her house, her long hair rippling over her shoulders like a black shawl. In spite of the heat she was wearing a full red skirt that came almost to her bare feet. At Carrot's expression she rocked back on her feet and laughed, her necklaces clicking on each other. "Not you," she said to Carrot, slapping her hip. "Her." She picked up a pebble and threw it at Tattoo, and the goat moved off toward the willow with a tomato in her mouth.

"Miserable critter," she said, shaking her head. "One of these nights there's going to be goat stew on the menu." She came to the wagon and picked up the bag of tomatoes and two heads of cabbage. She looked at Babe. "Might's well get started, Mr. Eggs. I'm anxious for my water. Come on," she said to Carrot.

Carrot watched Babe pick up the shovels and disappear around the corner of the house. She wished Ruby Dodd had asked him to carry in the groceries. He was about fifty times stronger than Carrot. Besides, Carrot had to get going. The green beans were choked with weeds. She waited a minute longer to see if Ruby Dodd would come back for the rest of it, then, sighing, she picked up the bags and followed her.

It smelled bad inside, hot and stale and something else. Like smelly socks. Carrot set the bags on a black table that was littered with playing cards. Ruby was standing at the sink making a great noise of lifting a bunch of pots out of the way so she could fill her teakettle. Carrot looked away, surveying the big room. In one corner, at the back, was a small bed covered with a bright quilt of black squares, stitched with red and pink diamonds. The bed was neatly made but the rest of the room was a jumble of pots and pans and dishes in the sink, on the counter, and even on the floor. Overhead, a million things hung from the rafters: pieces of brightly colored cloth, strings of shells, silver bird chimes, and bells of all sizes—cow bells, jingle bells, and clear glass bells with colored clappers. Her eyes were drawn back to the quilt.

Ruby Dodd had turned around. "Yep," she said, "your grandma made that." She pushed a cup of tea around the produce bags toward Carrot and sat down, motioning Carrot to do the same. "How is Clara?"

"She's got a cold," Carrot said, wondering why Gram would have made Ruby Dodd a quilt. Gram thought Ruby Dodd was a slovenly woman who didn't know enough to bring her wash in out of the rain.

"It's the goat cheese you smell," Ruby Dodd said. "It's been sittin' up all morning. Smells almost as bad as the goat, don't it?"

Carrot stood there holding on to the back of a chair, not going and not wanting to stay. She wished Ruby Dodd would have to go to the bathroom so she could escape. "I better get going," she said.

"It come by way of your father, that quilt," she said, stirring her tea with a tiny silver spoon.

Carrot blinked and stared at Ruby Dodd and then looked quickly away, at the rings on her fingers—seven of them, in silver and gold with brightly colored stones. She shifted from one foot to the other. Then she pulled out the chair and sat down. In the hot, smelly room, hunched over a steaming cup of tea, Carrot's teeth started to chatter. She was so embarrassed that she took a sip of tea and managed to slop it all over the playing cards. "Oops," she said, putting down the cup and spilling more tea. She pulled out the bottom of her T-shirt and started mopping at the table.

Ruby Dodd laughed. Not a snort, like Gram, or a giggle,

like her mother, but a deep, rolling kind of laugh, like she knew everything there was to know in the universe. "You're like him," she said, reaching across the table to take Carrot's hand.

Carrot wanted to take her hand away. She was afraid Ruby Dodd was going to try and read her palm. But she wanted to know about Ruby Dodd and her father. She didn't say a word while Ruby stroked her hand, with all her rings bumping across Carrot's palm.

"I guess I like to think he give it to me but he just wrapped me up in it. And I never give it back. Twenty-one years. I guess your Gram has stopped missing that quilt a long time ago." She let out a low chuckle.

Now Carrot looked at Ruby Dodd, at her wide, smooth face and smoky, almost black, eyes with heavy brows that went up like wings at the end. She didn't wear any makeup and her black hair looked like a big oriole's nest. Did she mean that she and her father were girlfriend and boyfriend?

"I know it was hard for you, losing Jesse like that." She crossed her hands over her breasts. "I mean I *know* it. I lost him, too. Only a long time ago." She grinned. "And it's a damn good thing for you I did." She patted Carrot's hand and gave it back to her. "You be off now. It's gonna storm and they'll be no one to bring you a dry blanket if you get soaked. Like they was for me."

Carrot stood up and then she hesitated. She rubbed the back of her leg with her other foot.

"Say it, girl," Ruby Dodd said, leaning forward and fixing Carrot with her smoky eyes.

"Wh-what did you mean?" Carrot asked in almost a

whisper. She didn't want to go on. She wanted Ruby Dodd to guess the rest of it.

Ruby Dodd reached up over her head and grabbed a leather thong attached to the clapper of an old metal bell. "Ring it out," she shouted over the ringing of the bell. "Sing it out."

"The killing part," Carrot murmured. "What you said about the killing part."

"Ahh, that." Ruby Dodd let go of the bell. "It's only a deer." She pointed at Carrot. "Just like your daddy, shooting a deer."

Carrot's hands flew to her face. "No! I'll never kill a deer. That's not true."

Ruby Dodd just nodded. "And your family will be glad for that venison this winter of all winters." She lifted a finger. "Wait. I'll get you a dried holly for your grandma. Holly has the highest wanting-to-do force of all the remedies. Just bind it to any part of her body. Powerful," she said, lifting her red skirt and stepping up on the chair and then on the table, planting her feet between the teacups and the vegetables. And she started untying a bunch of greenery from among the rags and doo dads.

Carrot looked at Ruby Dodd's big, dirty feet in the middle of the table and hated them. She hated Ruby Dodd for her messy house and for loving her father and most of all for her lies. She caught the spiky little holly sprig as it fell and she turned and went out the door without even saying good-bye, without even collecting the six dollars for the vegetables. She ran down the drive without looking back over her shoulder at Babe, digging just beyond the clotheslines.

131

She turned onto Bentley and the sun blasted her full in the face. As she ran the dry, vibrating buzz of cicadas felt like it was coming from inside her head. Her throat felt full of dust, and sweat ran down into her eyes. She stopped to wipe her face with her T-shirt and suddenly was too weary to run anymore. Taking a deep breath she started moving slowly down the road.

Why had she gone to Ruby Dodd's? She had known it was going to be a mistake. Gram was right about her. She was a slovenly woman who let goats run through her house. Only a weirdo would have shells hanging from her ceiling. And leaves. She looked down at the piece of holly that Ruby Dodd had untied for Gram. Stupid. She pitched it into the bushes. Lies. Her father would never love anyone like that. And Carrot, Carrot would never, in a million years, shoot a deer. How could Ruby Dodd think that someone who loved animals as much as she did would kill a deer? Even if her family were all starving she wouldn't do it. She would steal food from the grocery store before she would ever kill a deer. Ruby Dodd was off her rocker and she was going to tell Babe not ever to go back there, ever. Not even to finish the well.

She stopped to pick a vivid green fern and began fanning her face as she walked along. Suddenly a quick breeze rustled around her, drying the sweat on her hot forehead. She looked up and saw that the white, hot sky had filled with wind clouds, and behind, looming high and dark and threatening, were black ones rushing toward the sun. She realized the cicadas had stopped buzzing and there was an eerie silence all around her. It was going to storm. She would have to run the mile and a half back to Gram's. As she ran the wind picked up and the sun disappeared. The first raindrop hit her face, cool as lemonade. Ahead, down the road, she could see it coming, sweeping across McKenzie's field like a great silver sheet stretched taut. As the rain pounded over the road its smell rose in her nostrils, moist and pungent as new grass. Along the shoulders the dust began to explode in small puffs as the fat raindrops hit the ground. The sheet of rain hit her right at the McKenzie mailbox and soaked her in minutes, but the coolness felt so good she lifted her face as she ran. Behind her she heard the thunder, rumbling softly at first and then loud as a locomotive.

In the dark woods ahead she saw the jagged split in the sky, quick as an eyeblink. The thunder clapped so loudly that she felt she had been slammed into a dark closet. Suddenly there was a flash of lightning so close to her that it made the hair on her arms stand up. Carrot fell to her knees and hugged herself into a wet little ball the way her father had taught her to do. The noise that followed was like the end of the world, a clap of thunder so loud that she toppled over in the road like a frog.

She didn't even have time to pick herself up when the deer flew out of the woods. It seemed to come, like a frightened bird, from the air, and it leaped over her so that all she saw was its white underbelly and its four scrambling hooves sailing over her face. Neither did she see where it went. It appeared and it disappeared, leaving only the electricity of its panic in the air around her.

This was no time to sit in the road and think. She scrambled to her feet and started running for Gram's.

15

She couldn't get it out of her head. She dreamed worse dreams, nightmares about shooting the deer, about having the entire woods blow up in her face, dreams that woke her, sobbing and curled up to Beaut. The deer in the storm leaped out at her over and over, in her dreams and in her memory. Her life was made even worse by Gram. In all the time she had known her Carrot had never seen Gram take to her bed except to sleep. Now she had been in bed, coughing, for almost a week.

Carrot took in her dinners on a tray and sat with her while she ate what her mother had prepared. At the beginning of the week Gram had sat up quietly, staring at the old green fan that blew her gray frizz back from her forehead. But as soon as Carrot set down the tray she would point at anything unfamiliar and demand to know what Susan was feeding her. "Kiwi!" she would snort, plucking the offensive thing off her plate and dropping it in the wastebasket. "It sounds like something she got at the zoo."

But later in the week Gram barely noticed what was on

her plate. "This is squash blossom, Gram." Carrot pointed to a thin golden puff next to the scrambled eggs. "Mom thought it would make your food look more cheerful." To Carrot's dismay Gram didn't toss it in the basket; she didn't even snort. She coughed and pushed the food away. "I'm not hungry. It's too hot out."

"Please, Gram," Carrot pleaded. "Please eat something."

"All right. I'll eat the toast." She waved her hand for Carrot to take the rest away.

Carrot stood there, knowing if Gram didn't eat something, she wouldn't get better.

Gram looked at her with a little of the old snap and said for the dozenth time, "And *don't* call that fool doctor. I'd sooner have the man in the moon looking down my pipes."

As Gram worsened Carrot and her mom huddled in the kitchen whispering about her condition. "Maybe you should call the doctor," Carrot whispered, "she barely ate one bite of toast."

Her mother held her fist up to her mouth, her eyes wide with worry. "When I braided her hair this morning she made me promise not to call the doctor. 'The fool doctor,' she called him. I'm afraid," she murmured.

Carrot understood that her mother meant she was afraid of Gram, afraid to cross her in any way. Gram was a strong, outspoken woman and her mother was timid. She suddenly realized that her mother had always been afraid of Gram and that maybe that was why she hadn't liked coming here. Now Carrot wasn't sure if her grandmother was right or wrong. Couldn't the doctor give her some medicine to stop the coughing at least?

135

It was hard to carry on with Gram in bed and Beaut at work and Babe at Ruby Dodd's all week. That left just her mother to clean, cook, do the laundry, and run the house, and Carrot to take care of the garden and the chicks and the produce stand. In the mornings she and her mother would go down to the kitchen early. While her mother fixed breakfast for Babe and Beaut, Carrot packed them sack lunches—four sandwiches for Babe, one for Beaut. Carrot knew Beaut was embarrassed to carry a brown-bag lunch when all of the other employees at Lisanne's went to the Cube for a club sandwich or a hamburger and fries. But it would be ridiculous to spend three dollars a day on lunch when she could bring it for nothing. And almost every day Beaut took in bags of tomatoes and corn and other vegetables to sell to the ladies she worked with and even to some of the customers.

"You're turning into a marvelous saleswoman," her mother said, as she and Carrot helped Beaut load Gram's car with bags of vegetables.

"I should open a shop," Beaut said, rolling down the car window. "Bras and Cucumbers."

"Tomatoes and Girdles," Carrot yelled as Beaut backed down the drive. She smiled at her mother. "At least the garden is going well. I can barely keep up with the zucchini." She looked off behind the house at the full greenness of the half acre, now at its very peak. "Well," she said, moving toward it.

"Come back and have some breakfast," her mother said.

Carrot pulled a banana out of her pocket and waved it at her mother as she crossed the yard.

136

"Would you like me to bring you some coffee?" her mother called after her.

Carrot shook her head and picked up the hoe by the shed.

"Carrie—"

She looked back at her mother standing small and alone, a small breeze lifting her hair.

"You work too hard," her mother called.

Carrot kept walking to the garden but felt a small shock go through her body. Her mother wanted Carrot to come back to the house for company. She wanted to sit at the table and drink coffee with her the way she had done with her friends in Regal. Carrot almost dropped the hoe and went back to her. But there were ten rows to hoe and all the picking. And her mother couldn't afford to sit and drink coffee, either—not with the laundry to do, the canning jars to scour, all her phoning to her Rainbow customers. And there was Gram to take care of.

As Carrot hoed the rich humus from the compost around the tomato plants, she felt a surge of pride at the abundance around her. She recalled the day Babe had been trying to tell her how he felt about the garden, how special it felt for the two of them to provide food for the entire family. She hadn't understood then but she did now. She felt good, right down to her toes, as she sat at the table watching everybody eating. She felt like a person with an occupation—Farmer Carissa Turvy. She even liked it when people at the stand admired the produce. "This is the tenderest lettuce I've seen all summer." It was like they were complimenting her—telling her she had rosy cheeks or a great smile. That was probably how Babe felt about Mr. Eggs, she thought with a twinge of guilt. Wiping her hands on her shorts she bent to pick a perfect red tomato and bit it, the juice running down her chin.

"Looks like I'm just in time. I brought you lunch."

Carrot turned and smiled at her mother. Since Gram had been sick she hadn't had the time to fuss with makeup or roll up her hair with fake flowers. She was wearing a stained apron over a T-shirt and shorts, and on her feet were a pair of Gram's clunky brown oxfords. When she saw Carrot looking at her feet, she giggled.

"I was afraid I would step in something when I fed the chickens."

"You?" Carrot pointed at her mother in amazement.

"Oh, well, I could hear them screeching and clucking, and Babe had left this ground-up stuff right by the back door so I just—I scurried in and scurried out. I just dumped the bowl in a heap in the chicken yard. Is that okay?"

Carrot laughed. "It's a good thing you got out of there before one of them took a bite out of your leg." She was secretly pleased that her mother had fed the chickens even if she hadn't done a textbook job of it. She was trying; she was trying a lot harder than she ever had before. Unwrapping her peanut butter and jelly sandwich, Carrot took a big bite. "Umm. Want some?" She held it out.

Her mother shook her head. "I've got to take Clara's lunch in to her and hang the wash and find the screw-ons for the canning jars and—" She looked at her watch. "It's twelve-thirty already."

"I'd better get out to the stand," Carrot said. "I'm supposed to be there by noon."

"It must be nice sitting there in the shade, chatting with customers all afternoon."

Carrot snorted. "You want to try it?"

Her mother didn't hesitate. "You want to feed Gram?"

Carrot shrugged. "Sure." She helped her mother carry the baskets of produce out to the road. "Keep most of this in the shade," she advised, "so it stays fresher. There's the money box, your price list. If you get stuck, you know where I am."

When she got inside Carrot poured a glass of orange juice and took it down the hall to Gram's bedroom. "Gram," she said softly, pushing open the door. The small room was dark and cool. Gram liked the curtains shut and the fan blowing on her night and day. "Gram?" she said louder. Gram slowly lifted her hand in greeting.

"Here's some juice."

Gram tried to sit up but started coughing so hard she fell back against her pillow. Carrot sat down on the chair next to the bed and leaned forward with the glass of juice. "Can you drink it like this, Gram?" She tipped the glass to Gram's dry lips, a sip at a time until it was gone. "There," she said, setting down the glass. "Now what would you like for lunch? Soup? Scrambled eggs?"

Gram let out a long, raspy sigh. "I told your mother—" She turned and glared at Carrot. Even in her weakened state Gram could be grouchy and impatient. Carrot realized that her mother hadn't wanted to sit at the produce stand all afternoon so much as she had wanted to get away from Gram. Nobody could make her eat, nobody was allowed to call the doctor, nobody could run her house the way she could.

But Carrot understood Gram's crabbiness. She knew how much Gram hated being sick, hated inactivity. For the first time in her life Carrot had a chance to help Gram and it made her feel important. She hooked her heels on the rung of the chair and smiled at Gram. "Everything's under control," she said. "Mom is running the produce stand. I'm going to clean up the kitchen. After I fix your lunch," she added.

Gram sighed again.

"But first I thought I'd read to you." She added quickly, "It's mostly to help me. It's for school." She didn't want Gram to think she thought she was an invalid who needed to be entertained. "*Moby-Dick*," she said, looking to see Gram's reaction.

Gram nodded faintly and sank back on her pillow. Carrot opened the book but could barely see the print. "Do you mind if I open the curtains?" Gram just sighed again so Carrot got up and pulled open the "Hundred and One Dalmatians" printed curtains and sat back down. Since she had no particular idea what was going on she just started reading where the book fell open.

"'Beyond the Duodecimo—'" She stopped and looked down at the footnote. "That means a certain kind of book, with twelve pages, Gram. Anyway, 'this system,'" she went on, "'does not proceed, inasmuch as the Porpoise is the smallest of whales. Above, you have all the leviathans'— that's whales, Gram—'of note. But there are a rabble of uncertain, fugitive, half-fabulous whales, which, as an

140

American whaleman, I know by reputation, but not personally. I shall enumerate them by their forecastle appellations—' Appellations means what they're called by, Gram."

Gram emitted a faint groan. Carrot paused and went on, "'For possibly such a list may be valuable to future investigators, who—'"

"Stop," Gram said.

Carrot looked at her.

"Terrible," Gram muttered.

"Terrible? You think it's terrible?" Carrot looked from Gram to *Moby-Dick* and back to Gram. All this time she had thought she was stupid for not understanding all the big words, for skipping all over trying to find the good parts. If *Moby-Dick* was too hard for Gram it was too hard for her. "Yeah," she said. "I think it's terrible, too." She clapped the book shut and shoved it under Gram's bed. Then she took off her cap and leaned toward the bed to catch the breeze from the fan.

"Want some sliced-up tomatoes?" she asked, patting Gram's shoulder.

Gram ignored the question. "Where's Babe?"

"He's at Ruby Dodd's, remember? Digging a well."

Gram mumbled something. Carrot couldn't understand but she wanted to know. She wanted to know what Gram thought of Ruby Dodd. "What did you say, Gram?" She leaned over the bed but Gram didn't make a sound. "Gram?" she said, jiggling the bed. "Gram—Ruby Dodd has your quilt."

Gram's eyes opened and she turned to look at Carrot.

"The black one," Carrot said, "with the pink diamonds."

"Jesse—" Gram started coughing again. She coughed so hard the bed shook. Carrot opened the bottle of red syrup and poured some into a clear plastic cup and held it to Gram's lips. When Gram lay back Carrot asked, "Did my dad—was he her boyfriend?"

Gram held her hands against her chest and nodded.

So it was true. Carrot's cheeks burned. Why would her father love someone who wore seashell necklaces and dirty skirts and whose house looked like a hurricane? "But why?" she asked.

Gram didn't answer.

"Did she—did she cast a spell over him?"

Gram snorted. It was like her old snort. "She had her ways," she said in a raspy whisper.

Carrot stood up and leaned over the bed and looked into Gram's worn face. "Is she magic? Is Ruby Dodd magic?"

Gram shook her head.

"Well, but can she make you do things—things you don't want to do?"

Gram lifted her hand to Carrot's face. It felt hot and dry against her cheek. "Carrot—nobody can make you do what you don't want to. Nobody."

Carrot breathed a deep sigh and squeezed Gram's hand. "I'm going to fix you some lunch now, Gram. Just a little soup and toast."

For the rest of the afternoon Carrot happily bustled around the kitchen, scrubbing pans, running vinegar water over the counters the way Gram did, getting the canning jars up from the basement and washing them in hot sudsy water. She heated Gram some vegetable beef broth and made some dry toast, but when she took it in Gram was sleeping. She was sitting up in bed with two pillows behind her and the fan blowing back tendrils of her gray hair. Carrot could tell she was sound asleep by the steady rasping of her breath.

She sat by the bed all afternoon and watched over Gram. That's how she saw herself, like a nurse watching over her patient. She was worried about Gram but there was this little ripple of joy in her heart. She felt like she had been let out of prison. Nobody could make her do what she didn't want to do. Nobody could make her kill a deer. Not even Ruby Dodd.

Sometime before dinner Babe came home. "How's Mama?" he asked, sticking his head in the bedroom door.

"She's sleeping," Carrot whispered. She saw Babe glance at the uneaten tray of food next to the bed. "I'll take that out," Carrot said. "It's time for me to start dinner, anyway." She stood up and stretched her legs, surprised at how stiff she was from sitting. "Did you finish the well?"

Babe nodded and put his hands against his head. "Mama?" He sat down in the chair and leaned forward, his hands over his ears, and started to rock.

"She's just sleeping," Carrot said, putting her arms around Babe's neck. "You stay with her. That will make her feel better. You can let me know when she wakes up and wants her dinner." Carrot said it to make him feel better. She didn't believe Gram was going to be asking anyone for anything. She picked up the tray and went out.

Her mother was back in the kitchen frying onions and chopping a big head of cabbage. "Just cut up that chicken from last night," she said to Carrot, "and add some mayonnaise. We'll have sandwiches. How's Gram?"

"She didn't eat a thing."

Just then Beaut walked in. "How's Gram?" she asked, kicking off her shoes.

Her mother shook her head.

"Well, did you call the doctor?" Beaut asked, putting her hands on her hips. "You can't let her starve to death in there."

Her mother looked at Carrot, her forehead creasing between her eyebrows. "What do you think?"

"She said don't do it at least a dozen times," Carrot said. "She'll be mad as a hornet."

"That would be a relief," her mother said. The onions started smoking in the pan and she rushed over and scooped up two handfuls of chopped cabbage and dumped it in. "I'd welcome it if she was her old crabby self."

"Yeah," Carrot agreed. "I hate it when she's so quiet. It gives me the creeps."

"So do you want me to call the doctor or what?" Beaut asked. She had picked up the phone book and was thumbing through the P's for Pawlowski. "Does he make house calls?"

"I don't know," her mother said. She had put her fist up to her mouth, so Carrot knew she was afraid. Was she afraid that Gram would be angry? Or that Gram was going to die?

Babe came into the kitchen. "She says are you trying to starve her to death?"

They all stared at him.

He grinned. "She says bring her whatever you have cooking, right now."

All four of them ran back down the hall into Gram's

bedroom. Sure enough, there she was sitting up in bed, looking cross.

"Well, for pity's sake," she said, "did you just come to stare at me? Didn't you even bring me a—a squash blossom?"

Carrot was the only one who noticed. She saw it stuck in Gram's braid after the others had rushed back to the kitchen. A sprig of holly.

16

"I can't get this last bolt out," Carrot said. "It's jammed. Are you going to keel over or anything?" She looked at Babe, who was holding up the whole roof of the produce stand with his arms and back. He reminded her of the guy in a mythology book at school, named Atlas, who held up the whole world on his shoulders.

"It's okay," Babe said. "It's not heavy."

"Not heavy for you maybe. I'd be smeared out like a squashed fly." She picked up a hammer from the grass and hit the bolt. "There. You can let it down now."

"It's a tragedy," she said, following behind Babe with the TURVY'S PRODUCE sign while he carried the entire roof to the shed. "How can it be fall already? I hate closing up the stand; I hate being back in school. I just want to be a farmer, Babe. I don't care about equilateral triangles and all that junk." She watched Babe's muscles ripple as he heaved the roof into the shed and propped it up against the wall.

"I wish I could," Babe said, wiping his hands across the belly of his shirt. "Learn about Saturday triangles."

She made a face. "They make you go up to the board and draw all these scratchy shapes and put degrees to go with them, and you have to add up all the degrees to make a hundred and eighty, and it's so boring you want to turn into a piece of chalk."

"I like that," Babe said, marching back to the road. "Go up in front of everyone and draw."

"Then *you* go to school and I'll stay home and feed the chickens."

Babe didn't say anything till they got back to what was left of the stand. He picked up a board and lifted it to his head. "I'm too stupid."

Carrot's face flushed with anger. "I told you not to say that."

"I'm not too stupid," he corrected himself. "I'm smart in other places. Carrot," he said, "remember when I carried Jesse home when he had a broken leg?"

"Tell me again," she said, even though her father had told her lots of times about what had happened when he and Babe were boys and had jumped off a railroad trestle into the Tittabawassee River. "Jesse jumped first and then me," Babe said. "But I came up and Jesse didn't come up. He hit a rock, that's what broke his leg."

"Did you bring him up?" Carrot pictured Babe at age twelve, searching underwater for his fourteen-year-old brother.

Babe nodded. "I dragged him under my arm to the shore and then he woke up and started to holler all right. 'Cause

147

his leg hurt so bad. He screamed bloody murder all the time I was carryin' him home."

"Wow." Carrot stared at Babe standing there with a huge piece of siding on his head. "You saved my dad's life."

"Yeah," Babe said.

"You're a hero."

"I know," Babe said.

They loaded the last of the stand into the shed and walked back to the road. The grass was all matted and yellow where the stand had been all summer. There were still cucumbers and zucchini piled up on a canvas tarp, but they looked forlorn. Nobody would buy them now.

Babe sat down in his folding chair. "I miss Jesse," he said, resting his elbows on his knees and sinking his head into his hands.

Carrot sat down on the grass and draped one arm over Bing, the tin deer. Neither of them said anything for a few minutes. They sat there watching the traffic go by. "Say some more," Carrot said, "about when he was a kid."

"He played the Army Band mouth organ and I sang, 'Daisy, Daisy' outside the Cracker Bar and all the peoples gave us money. Then Mama came and whupped us."

Carrot laughed. "What for?"

Babe scratched his head. "I forget."

"Was he jokey and friendly like Beaut or was he sort of like—like me?"

"Oh . . ." Babe thought. "He was just Jesse." He sighed. After a moment he whispered to Carrot, "Where is he?"

She turned to look at Babe. "What do you mean? You know where he is."

Babe looked down at his shoes. "Dead."

Carrot nodded.

"Wh-where is that?" he whispered.

Carrot thought about the cold March day, how the heels of her shoes sank into the spongy earth when she walked away from everybody, away from the big hole in the ground so she wouldn't have to see. The big gray box with the red roses and silver letters that said, "To Dad." The flowers, the gray box, everything into the ground. "I—I don't know," Carrot said. "I don't know where it is." She took the John Deere cap off Bing and sailed it like a Frisbee into the air. They had long since tossed out the red T-shirt and tennis shoes from the Horning boys. Now she bent over and picked up a stone. Turning, she hurled it with all her might at Bing, making a loud whang. The tin deer swung back and forth, catching and releasing the low afternoon sunlight. *"Wha-aaang!"* Another stone came from behind her and struck Bing dead center. She whirled around.

"What are you two loafing for?" Dan Durbin stood there in a Rocky and Bullwinkle T-shirt, grinning at her. He stooped over and picked up the red cap she had sailed into the air and put it on. "What else are you giving away?"

"You want some—some zucchini and some cucumbers?" Babe pointed at the tarp. "Take 'em. Take 'em all. Mama says she's tired of pickling."

Dan hooked his thumbs in his jeans pockets and looked down at Carrot. "We're closing the Dairy Delite too. This is your last day for a Velvet Thundercloud. Hey—since you don't have to mind the store, why not bike with me into town? I'll fix you the swan song of Velvet Thunderclouds."

149

One at a time, he pelted pebbles at Bing, making a steady pinging noise as he talked.

"Lemme get my bike. C'mon, Carrot, let's go. I'm gonna tell Mama we're going for ice cream."

Carrot put out her hand. "No, Babe. We've got Mr. Eggs to deliver."

"Oh boy, oh boy." Babe slapped the side of his head. "How could I forget? The chicks are laying, Dan. We got— umm—we got, how many eggs, Carrot?"

"Sixty this week." She had scooped up some pebbles and stood behind Dan, hitting Bing directly in the red circle.

"Oops," he said, looking over his shoulder. "I forgot you were Annie Oakley."

Carrot cringed. She had hoped everyone at school had forgotten about the squirrel. She dumped the pebbles and went over and started loading the zucchini into a bushel basket.

"Did you mean that about the zucchini?" Dan looked at Carrot. "My old man loves zucchini. Zucchini bread, fried zucchini, zucchini and eggs." He shrugged. "He doesn't even live with us but he comes over for dinner every Sunday."

Carrot stared at him.

"Weird, huh?" he said cheerfully, picking out two huge zucchini.

"Take a bunch of little ones. They're more tender." She handed him five small zucchini.

"My parents are divorced, and my older brother lives with him and my sister and I live with my mother. And we've been eating Sunday dinner together every week for three years."

"Why are you telling me?" Carrot asked, amazed that he could talk so freely about something so personal.

"I don't know." He laughed. "I talk too much when I'm nervous. I just want to say I'm sorry about—about your father. Dying," he added.

"He was my brother," Babe said. "His name was Jesse."

"Yeah?" Dan looked at him. "Well, he must have been a great guy, Babe."

"Yeah," Babe said. "He's dead."

Dan nodded. "Thanks for the zucchini," he said to Carrot. "Listen, you know that—that—do you want to go to the Homecoming Dance with me?"

"Dance?" she echoed. "No, I can't," she blurted out, wondering why in the world he was asking her to a dance. Just because she gave him some zucchini?

"Okay," he said. "Well, so long. See you in Smoznak's class."

She watched him bike down the road, the bag of zucchini swinging off his handlebar. She sensed Babe watching her. "What are you staring at?"

"He didn't want me to go to the Dairy Delite," Babe pouted. "He only wanted you."

"Gimme a break, Babe." She started heaving zucchini and cukes into the basket. Now she supposed it was going to be touchy sitting right next to him in English. Yech. When she had first gone into English a week ago she couldn't believe she had Smoznak again. There she was, sitting on the edge of her desk in a bright red dress and red lipstick and her hair in a new, over-the-eyebrow style. Carrot had expected to maybe wave at her in the halls once in a while but never to get into a real conversation with her. Of course, even while the kids were streaming into the classroom and Mrs. Smoznak was calling out hello to everyone and drawing up a seating chart at the same time, she still remembered to ask about *Moby-Dick*. "Did you finish it?" she asked, smiling her big smile that reminded Carrot of wax Halloween lips.

Carrot shook her head.

"It *is* long," Mrs. Smoznak agreed. "Did you get to the Candles chapter?" Without waiting for Carrot's answer she raised her arm. "'Whencesoe'er I came; wheresoe'er I go; yet while I earthly live, the queenly personality lives in me, and feels her royal rights.'"

Carrot shook her head, embarrassed to be the cause of Mrs. Smoznak's transformation into a dramatic actress in front of the whole class. Mrs. Smoznak didn't seem to notice that a lot of the kids were snickering.

"Ahhh," she said, clasping her hands over her bosom, "you must promise me that you'll finish it."

Carrot stood there not wanting to lie but not ever wanting to open *Moby-Dick* again. "My grandmother thinks it's terrible," she muttered.

"Terrible?" For a second Carrot thought Mrs. Smoznak was going to be angry, but then she laughed. Her cheeks got pink and she laughed louder. "It *is* terrible. Yes," she said, "I guess it is."

Even though she didn't seem to be angry she made Carrot sit right in front of her. Which just happened to be next to Dan Durbin. She could almost feel him casting a

152

shadow over her entire right side. Always jiggling his skinny leg, whacking his pencil against his desk. Nervous. If he was so nervous, why didn't he keep his mouth shut? He should know she wasn't the type of person to go—

"Is he your boyfriend, Carrot? Is Dan Durbin your boyfriend?"

Carrot picked up a cucumber and threw it at Babe, whacking him in the back.

But Babe couldn't keep it to himself. After dinner her mother took her aside.

"I understand that nice boy asked you to the Homecoming Dance. I'm sure it was the same one who asked about you the afternoon I was at the stand." She brushed at Carrot's bangs while she talked, her voice all chirpy like she was going to sell Carrot some Luvlee Lashes.

"I'm not going, Mom."

"Surely you don't want to miss the Homecoming Dance? Why, Beaut is going. Gram's making her a lovely new dress and I'll bet she would make—"

"No."

"Listen, Carrie." She lowered her voice. "I haven't said anything before because I didn't want to hurt anyone's feelings. But you can't spend your life hiding out with a mentally retarded man. I mean Babe is sweet but he's not real. Do you know what I'm saying?"

"Yes," Carrot snapped. "I know what you're saying. But Babe *is* real. He's the realest, nicest, best friend I've ever had. And if you don't understand that, then you're the one who's retarded."

17

*C*arrot sat on the footstool under the moose and looked out the window. It hardly seemed possible that it was October, that summer's golden warmth was behind them. She watched the wind shake the maple tree, watched the flurry of red and gold tumbling through the bright sky. So many leaves had already fallen that she could see through the trees now, all the way down to the curve in the driveway. Back the other way, out the kitchen window, the whole woods were starting to open up. Beyond the cornfield she could see the slope of the hill clearer than at any time in the summer. She thought of how different the seasons were here than in Regal. There, it wasn't the outside world so much as it was a change inside the house. Her mother always took the floral print slipcovers off so that the sofas could go back to their dark green plaid. She brought in the potted geraniums from the back patio and her father took down the screens and put up the storm windows. Then the flannel pajamas and all the sweaters came down from the attic.

This was better, she thought, even if it did make her sad to see the leaves flying. More than any other season autumn made her think of her father. Tromping through the woods with him, kicking up dry leaves, laughing at some squirrel's last desperate rush to gather nuts.

"Honestly, Carrot, you don't have to wait through this whole long ordeal. I know you're anxious to get going." Beaut had just come down the stairs.

"Nonsense," her mother said to Beaut. "I'm sure when Carrie sees how ravishing you look she'll say yes to the next young man who asks her to a dance."

Carrot did think Beaut looked beautiful in the pink, cotton-candy dress that Gram had made. She also thought it was ridiculous to get all shined up with powder and curls and big earrings in the middle of the afternoon when the dance didn't even start until eight o'clock. But their mom wanted to take pictures and Andy's mom wanted to take pictures and then they had to go to some friends for appetizers and then to dinner. Carrot was glad she wasn't going. She would be exhausted before the dance even started. Besides, she'd much rather be out in the woods with Babe. And she couldn't stand to have her mother flapping around her like a nervous Henny Penny.

"Let me spritz a little more on top," she said. Carrot could smell the sickly sweet hair spray clear across the room.

"I hope he doesn't have the top down," Beaut worried.

"Just tell him to put it up," Carrot said. "If you don't want your hair to blow around."

"Oh, well," Beaut said, shrugging.

Carrot rolled her eyes. She couldn't imagine letting a boy push you around like that. Reluctantly, she got up when her mother nudged her over to the mantel with Beaut to have their picture taken.

"Now take your hat off, darling. And the jacket, please. I'm going to have that filthy thing cleaned, Carrie. Leave it there." She pointed at the sofa.

"Beauty and the Beast," Carrot said, baring her teeth at Beaut. She felt like a midget because Beaut was wearing tall, skinny heels to match her dress.

"All right," their mom said, "once more. And this time smile, Carrie."

"Oh, Babe," Beaut said, as he came in the back door, whooshing a blast of cool air at them. "Would you snap the three of us? All you do is focus and the picture comes out here."

Later, when she was in the woods with Babe, Carrot thought about the picture Babe had taken. They had stood and watched the faint figures come into focus. Her mom in the middle, one arm around each of them, smiling her tight little smile, no doubt worrying if Beaut was going to have a good time at her party and whether Mrs. Lyons was going to buy enough blusher and lipstick so she could make her quota, worrying about Gram working too hard even though she was perfectly healthy again, worrying about money, probably worrying about Carrot not wanting to go to the dance. Worrying like she always worried. And Beaut in her floating pink dress with her hair in soft waves around her shiny pink cheeks, too sweet for a dork like Andy but still looking just the way she always did. And Carrot, grubby as usual in her plaid flannel shirt with a button missing on the cuff and too-short blue jeans. Not so smiley as Beaut, not so nervous as her mother. She looked normal, too—her hair was shorter—but otherwise like herself. The picture would have been okay, even with her father missing, if it weren't for the moose. That awful, sad-eyed moose hung over their heads like a skull and crossbones. Mom should have made them stand in front of the refrigerator. What a family portrait, she thought, shuddering.

"—soons I finish there, she wants me to start another pile on the other side. Only maple. She only wants to burn maple. Because the oaks are something. They're, I think, they're holy. She don't burn oaks."

Carrot had been so lost in thought she didn't realize Babe had been talking to her. "Who?" she asked.

"Ruby Dodd. She's paying me twenty a cord. If I cut five that's how much?"

"A hundred dollars," she said. "Why do you have to do it? Why can't she get it delivered from the Christmas tree people?"

"A hundred dollars!" Babe clapped his hands. "A hundred dollars. I can make a hundred dollars and buy a cow. Mama said she wanted a cow for Christmas."

"A side of beef," Carrot said. "Roasts, hamburger, steak—food. That's what she meant." She didn't try to talk Babe out of doing odd jobs for Ruby Dodd but she no longer went with him when he was Mr. Eggs. She knew Babe adored Ruby. He was convinced that the holly he had put in Gram's braid had cured her even though Gram scoffed at the idea. "I just got my appetite back is what happened," she said. That's what Carrot thought, too. But there was something weird about Ruby Dodd that made Carrot want to stay away.

"Here?" Babe asked, setting Bing down in front of an embankment covered with bright yellow leaves. They had put up straw bales earlier in the day so that Carrot could do target practice while Babe was sawing wood for the winter from a lightning-struck tree on the other side of the marsh.

Carrot nodded and leaned her rifle against a log. She felt in the pocket of the canvas jacket for the cartridges. Her mom had been so busy with Beaut she hadn't seen Carrot put the jacket back on. She wouldn't feel right in the woods without it. "I'll come when I've used up my shells," she said, and watched Babe lumber through the leaves, the big ax over his shoulder. Even after he had disappeared through a tangle of orange bittersweet she could hear his movement through the leaves. *Crunch, crunch, crunch.* Like walking through a big bowl of corn-flakes. From the other direction she heard a shot. Somebody else, probably Gram's neighbor, Mr. McKenzie, was target shooting. Getting ready for the November hunt. Far overhead a flock of geese passed, gabbling. Through the trees she could see one part of their V, each bird like a pencil dot. Even after they disappeared she could hear their faint clamor. The echo stayed in her mind more than in her ears, tracing a little memory across her heart. She felt suddenly sick with loneliness. She wanted to run a hundred miles an hour through the woods, down the road, through the town, up Weenie Hill and down—run until her legs gave out, run until she couldn't think anymore, until she couldn't feel. She took a deep breath. Stupid. Don't ruin a perfect autumn day, she told herself.

Pulling a cartridge from her pocket she loaded the shotgun and lifted it to her shoulder, scoping Bing's red circle. The shot hit the target with a whang. First time, she thought proudly. She hadn't fired at the target in seven months. She stepped over the log and walked back another twenty feet to a patch of aspen and dewberry vines. Lifting her rifle to her shoulder she sighted again, faintly aware of the sun on the top of her head, the wind slapping leaves up against her legs. She squeezed the trigger just as something broke through the patch of wintergreen to the left of the embankment. Her shot went wide.

It was a big buck. Carrot lowered her gun and watched as the deer scrambled toward the short rise and struggled to climb it. Then she saw. In his right flank was a bullet wound that made the deer's hind leg dangle uselessly as his hooves clawed at the ground. She was so close she could hear his snorting breath as he scrambled to get a footing. Blood fell from the wound, spattering the yellow leaves with bright red. She felt a sudden sourness in her stomach like she was going to throw up. Babe, she thought, looking off to the right where he had gone. But what could Babe do? She could see that the deer was too weak even to climb the small bank. Too weak and in too much pain.

She watched the buck lose his precious footing and

159

slide backward, still thrusting forward with his big head. He stayed motionless for a moment, half up and half down, and in his helplessness he turned his head, heavy with a rack, and looked at her. He had known all along that she was there, another reason for his wild-eyed terror.

Carrot's heart was racing, pounding in her ears. "It's okay," she breathed, putting her hand out, wanting to run to the big buck as she had to the little fawn years ago. But she stayed huddled against the aspen, too frightened of the deer, of the big swinging rack. "Babe!" she cried, knowing he would never hear. "Help me," she whimpered.

It seemed as if she watched the deer for hours, doing his ugly three-legged dance in front of her—lurching and falling, lurching and falling. She made her eyes focus on the rough tan fur of his back, the soft white of his underbelly, white as snow. In her imagination she could see the buck bounding through the woods, quick as an arrow, his antlers held high. All grace and speed. She pictured him curling down in a winter thicket, his sleek belly full of acorns, waiting for spring, for tender shoots and green leaves. Maybe waiting for a little doe. She remembered how she and her father had seen a great buck like this courting a slender little doe, bounding after her around the pines and through the underbrush until he had chased her back to the very blind where they both sat watching. The little doe stopped long enough for the buck to nuzzle her and then bounded off again, quick as a heartbeat. She remembered how she and her father had laughed at the poor silly buck being teased by his true love. She wondered then if he had ever won the little doe.

She decided now that he had. He had fathered fawns in the springs and battled big antlered bucks in the autumns. This was the big old buck that always survived, the one her father trailed a dozen times, for hours, for days sometimes, and raised his rifle to as many times, and the buck always went free. Always.

She closed her eyes, seeing the deer leap up and over the embankment, bounding away to the safety of the deepest woods, its tail like a proud, white flag. "Daddy," she whispered. "Daddy, please."

It was a prayer that he would take pity on the deer, take pity on her, make everything all right.

She opened her eyes and looked at the deer. He was down. His dark eyes stared back at her, full of wonder.

For the longest time Carrot didn't move either. "Big old buck," she said at last. "It's okay." She put her hand out, still wanting to stroke the slender nose, to soothe away pain and fear. She inched forward. "It's okay. I'm your friend. It's okay." She got within ten feet of the deer and he lifted his head from the ground. They looked at each other. "It's okay," she said, the tears starting.

She lifted her gun and fired.

Carrot crumpled to the ground. She didn't look at the hole in his flank or the other hole—the one she had made. "I'm your friend," she sobbed. She put her hands on the deer's white underbelly. It was soft and warm. How could he be dead—something that had been running through the woods only a short time ago, that had been looking at her

161

with frightened eyes only seconds ago. She buried her face in her hands and sobbed.

She didn't move when she heard twigs snapping. She sat there not caring that tears were running down her cheeks, that her nose was running.

"Well, lookee here. We got us a little girl *and* a big deer."

Carrot turned around to face Bert and Dudley Horning. She jumped up, her fists raised. "Idiots," she yelled.

"Now don't give us no trouble, honey," Bert said, his right eye twitching.

"You shot it out of season and you're trespassing on my grandmother's property."

"Now, Missy, just step aside," Dudley said, kicking at a log. "We'll just take this here deer and clear out. We don't want no trouble."

"*No!*" Carrot threw herself over the deer. "Get away from him."

Dudley and Bert started laughing and one of them reached down and grabbed her by the arm.

There was a sudden explosion of snapping branches to their right. A log sailed past her head and Babe came roaring through the brush like a grizzly bear. "Let her go!" he shouted. Carrot was instantly dropped. At the same moment she saw Dudley's feet come off the ground. Babe tossed him across the forest floor like a rag doll. With one big arm he grabbed him back up by the belt buckle and slammed him into a tree.

"Don't!" Dudley cried, raising his arms in front of his face.

Babe punched him in the belly and drew back for another blow, when he saw Bert sneaking away through the woods. He dropped Dudley and shot after Bert, grabbing him by the seat of his pants.

"No!" Bert screamed, just before Babe's fist connected with his chin. Babe wound up again. "Please," Bert whimpered.

"Get outa here!" Babe roared. "And stay outa here!"

Bert nodded wildly, his mouth bleeding. "Just let us," he pleaded.

"I'll smash you!" Babe cocked his fist again.

Bert held up his hands. "Don't, Babe. Ohpleaseohplease. We won't bother you anymore. Just let us go." He looked at his brother lying on the ground. Dudley groaned and nodded. "Please," Dudley echoed, but it came out like "pweeze," because of his mashed lip.

Babe dragged Bert by the collar over to where Dudley was, and dropped him next to his brother. "Git," he hissed.

The Horning boys scrambled to their feet and only paused to look back at their rifles. Carrot had dragged both guns over to the stump where she sat.

"Git!" Babe yelled again, and they didn't look back. They limped back through the brush in the direction they had come.

"Wait!" Babe roared.

The brothers turned, clinging to each other, their faces wide with terror.

"Pay up the money."

The brothers looked from Babe to Carrot.

"Five dollars," Carrot said, glaring back at them.

They didn't question it. They reached into their pockets

163

and held out money to Babe, who snatched it without a word. "Git outa here," Babe said, kicking at the ground for emphasis. And they went.

Then Babe came and sat on the ground beside her and Carrot put her arms around his neck and wept.

18

*C*arrot slept fitfully, groaning and sliding closer to Beaut and then dropping off to sleep again. Outside, the wind howled like a hungry wolf and rain pelted the windows. Then Carrot heard an even eerier sound, a sound that yanked her straight up in bed. It was the old brass bell at the corner of the house, the one Gram rang when her father shot a deer. Gram wouldn't ring it now, in the middle of the night. What thing, what ghost, was out there making the deep clanging sweep through the night?

"Beaut, wake up," Carrot whispered, sliding to the other side of the bed. But there was no one there.

"Beaut," she whimpered, looking around the room, as if Beaut might be hiding in a dark corner. She shut her eyes and put her hands over her ears, trying to block the sound of the bell, the memory, the smell of death. But she could still hear the ringing, still see the tortured struggle of the deer. The deer that Ruby Dodd had told her she would kill.

She opened her eyes. "I shot it," she whispered to the darkness. "I killed the deer." The words struck her heart like a heavy blow. She pressed the heels of her palms into her eye sockets and felt the hot tears. She was all alone, the most miserable person in the world. She felt broken, like a little shell that someone had crushed into a million pieces. There was no one to fix her, no one to comfort her.

Her father would have understood. She pictured herself running from the woods into his waiting arms. "I killed the deer, Daddy. I didn't want to shoot it but I did it. It's back there lying in the woods, its beautiful head in the dust." She smelled his piney, woodsy smell, felt the rough wool of his shirt against her cheek, the strength of his arms wrapping around her, holding her until the pain dissolved into a tiny, bitter lump—something she could bear if he would only share it with her. A wave of longing for her father swept over her. For his slow and easy smile, the slope of his shoulders, the way his big body bounced when he walked ahead of her. And his silence, his deep, listening silence when she had something to tell him.

Carrot put her arms around herself and rocked like Babe rocked when he was upset. She rocked and she rocked but it didn't help. She felt like a baby chick out in the rainstorm, far from Henny Penny. She didn't hear her mother come in, didn't know she was there till she felt her touch on her arm.

"Carrie?"

Carrot stopped rocking and lifted her head.

"What is it, why are you crying?" She sat on Beaut's side of the bed and brushed at Carrot's bangs.

Carrot drew in a ragged breath and shook her head, not trusting her voice.

"Is it the deer? Is that why you're upset?"

"Yes." Carrot snuffed loudly. "No—" She wiped at her face. "Where's Beaut?"

"She's still at the party, I suppose. Dancing the night away. I hope that boy puts the top up in this storm. She'll ruin her new dress."

Oddly, it was calming to hear her mother worrying about Beaut's dress. Life was still going on in her mother's world, in Beaut's world. "M-mom," she said. "Do you hear that—that sound?"

Her mother stopped fussing with Carrot's hair and tipped her head. "It's just that old bell, Carrie. Nothing amazing about that. Not in this storm."

"It makes me think of the deer. That it's ringing because I—because of that."

Her mother caught Carrot's hand. "Ghosts, you mean?" She laughed and shook her head. "It's just the wild, wild wind." She began rubbing Carrot's hand like it was cold. "Mercy, Carrie, you've looked like a little white-faced ghost yourself ever since you came back from the woods." She folded up Carrot's hand into a little ball and ran her fingers over the knuckles. "Daffy down, dilly up, coffee brown, in your cup. Remember?"

Carrot nodded. Her mother used to say the rhyme up and down her knuckles when she was little, getting her ready for bed. "I didn't want to do it, Mom," she said in a quavery voice. "I never wanted to, ever. When Ruby Dodd told me I would shoot the deer I should never have picked up my gun again. I should never have gone in the woods. How did she know, Mom? How did she know I would do it?"

"Sssst. She's a crazy lady, Carrie, who never washes her

167

feet. She's full of ideas and crazy spells. And singing." She sighed. "I'm not saying that she can't forecast the future. Nor am I saying that she can. I'm saying that there is nothing so enticing about her." She paused. "Some people may think so. I am not one of them."

"But she made me. I didn't want to kill the deer. She made me."

Now her mother spoke sharply. "You're just overwrought, Carrie. That woman didn't make you do a thing. You have brains. You have a free will. You could have put that gun down and walked away. Just turned and walked away from that poor old deer."

"No," Carrot said. "I couldn't. He was suffering."

"Then you didn't want to. Simple as that." She snapped her fingers.

"I *did* want to. I wanted to walk away but something told me—"

"It wasn't Ruby Dodd, I promise you."

Carrot was silent. Something rose in her like a little flicker of light, something she wanted to see but couldn't. She waited until she saw the face, the easy, so familiar, beloved face. "No," she said. Again, the deepest wave of longing passed over her, like the homesickness of a lost child. But with it came understanding. Now she remembered what had happened. She looked at her mother, at her gentle, moonlit beauty in the little room, and she withdrew her hand. She wanted to keep what she knew, what she understood, all to herself. Between her and the one she loved best.

"What, Carrie? What is it?"

Carrot shook her head and lay down. "I just want to go back to sleep."

"But, sweetheart—"

"G'night, Mom."

Carrot watched her mother move toward the door in the darkness. Away from her. Safely away from her. Her mother wouldn't understand anyway. She never understood. Not like her father. Keep it inside. Just keep it inside. Like a bucket of tears. That bucket she had been carrying so long she thought her bones would crack. As her mother disappeared she felt the cracking, but it wasn't in her bones. It was in her heart.

"Mom—"

Her mother hurried back into the room. "I just knew there was something." She sat on the side of the bed and leaned toward Carrot. "What, Carrie?"

"It was Dad that told me to do it. That's why I didn't walk away. Mom, I was so scared watching the deer bleeding and struggling to get up. I was more scared than I've ever been in my life. I didn't want to be the one to kill it— I wanted to run away but I couldn't move. I couldn't think. So I prayed to Dad to help me."

"And—and your father, he—he told you to shoot it?" her mother asked, squeezing the words out, one at a time.

Carrot shook her head. "He said, 'There's nothing to be afraid of, Carrot.'" She paused, still hearing her father's words echoing in her mind. Then she looked at her mother. "So I wasn't afraid. And I pulled the trigger."

"Oh." Her mother hung her head. "Your poor father," she whispered.

Carrot stared at her mother, realizing for the first time how much she was hurting. "Do you still miss him?"

"Oh, Carrie. I'm like an old, withered nosegay. I feel ugly and I feel useless. Every night when I go to bed I play a little—oh, just a silly game, that my—that he will be waiting for me." She thumped the mattress with her hand. "I could have been different. If I'd had more time."

Carrot picked up her mother's arm and pulled it around her. "I play that game, too. I pretend Babe is Dad."

Her mother gave a bitter laugh. "If he could only see us, how foolish we are."

"Mom, he talked to me. Just like you're talking to me."

"Maybe," she said, pulling Carrot closer. "Maybe he *was* the reason you shot that old deer. It doesn't even matter, you know? That deer, that dead deer, I don't even care anymore."

Carrot looked at her mother in amazement.

"It just doesn't pierce me to the quick, like before," she said. "I see the world differently out here on the farm. In the cold weather all the tomato plants shrivel up, the zucchini, the green beans, everything dies. But next year I know you and Babe will plant another garden. Death is always going to happen. You just have to keep planting seeds." She looked at Carrot. "I hope that old deer planted a fawn somewhere along the way."

Carrot nodded.

"And I don't blame your father—not anymore. I'm finally starting to understand him." She gave a short laugh. "A little late."

They sat in an easy silence for a few moments. Then her mother started humming.

It was one of Babe's songs and Carrot sang the words. "'Tis the gift to be simple, 'tis the gift to be free—"

"Hey, what are you guys doing?" Beaut switched on the bedroom light and stood there in her wet, pink, party dress, staring at them.

"'Tis the gift to come down, where you ought to be." Their song drowned out the howling wind and the ringing bell and the everlasting fury of the rain.

19

"**H**appy birthday, to you—happy birthday to you—happy birthday, dear Carissa Alyssa—happy birthday to you-u-u."

Beaut stopped singing and got out of bed. She opened the side of the pie safe where she kept her sweaters and took out a small, wrapped present. "Here," she said. "I thought it would be better to give this to you now."

"Thanks, Beaut." Carrot unwrapped the box, lobbing the ball of silver wrapping paper into the wastebasket. When she took off the lid she groaned, and held up the pink lacy bra from Lisanne's Lingerie. "What am I supposed to do with this?"

"The same thing you do with your ratty old gray bras, silly. It's not like everyone can see it. Carrot, there's nothing wrong with wearing a pretty bra."

Carrot laughed. "Well, at least you didn't give it to me over dinner. Thanks, Beaut." She hugged her sister and jumped out of bed, squealing at the feel of the ice-cold floor against her bare feet. It was only November sixteenth and there was already a skiff of snow on the ground.

When Beaut came back from her shower Carrot smoothed down her sweatshirt. "Can you tell?" She held out her arms.

Beaut rolled her eyes. "Do you think I have X-ray vision? Relax. You look perfectly normal."

On the school bus Beaut took a seat with Nicole, so Carrot sat across the aisle, next to a girl named Frannie. "Did you turn in your essay?" she asked Carrot.

"Yeah," Carrot said. "She doesn't make it easy, does she?"

"Oh, I don't know," said Frannie. "I thought it was cinchy. I wrote about the family reunion we have every year on my mother's side—the Carters? We all sit around for five hours in the sweltering heat and stuff ourselves with greasy chicken and Foo Foo Eggs—that's my uncle's secret recipe for deviled eggs. The highlight of the day is when all the kids line up and get measured against the back of the garage. Every year, 'Line up, kids. Time to get measured!'" She imitated someone with a megaphone.

Carrot laughed. "Boring."

"Exactly. That's my subject. Boredom."

Carrot hoped Frannie wouldn't ask what her subject was. She wasn't sure she had done it right. She should have made hers funny like Frannie's. Just then they passed the cows, and the eighth-grade boys leaned against the windows and started mooing.

Carrot grinned at Frannie. "Some things never change."

She was walking into English with Frannie when Dan

Durbin came up from behind and stuck his finger in the middle of her back.

"Hey!" Carrot's cheeks flamed. She was sure the gesture had something to do with the pink bra she was wearing.

Dan held up his hands. "Sorry," he said. "Just my oafish way of saying hello. Don't freak out."

Carrot tugged at her sweatshirt and sat down, studying her fingernails.

Mrs. Smoznak came in and wrote on the blackboard: "Why not go out on a limb? That's where all the fruit is." Then she walked around to the front of her desk and sat on it. "Any world records for today?"

Drew, a boy who always wore his overalls unfastened on one shoulder, raised his hand. "My mother burned, I mean really fried, three grilled sandwiches in a row last night."

Mrs. Smoznak laughed. "Did you eat them?"

"Heck, no. My dad called up and ordered pizza."

"I had an evening like that, too," Mrs. Smoznak said. "I put the kettle on and forgot it when I went to answer the phone, and the water boiled away and scorched the kettle and finally the smoke alarm went off."

Carrot smiled. She thought about the time she set a bag of tomatoes too near the road and a car pulled up and turned them into tomato juice.

"There are some other world records," Mrs. Smoznak said, holding up a stack of papers. "You wrote some excellent essays covering every possible emotion—love, hate, greed, even boredom. Anyone want to volunteer to read his or her essay?" She looked around. Nobody volunteered. "Okay," she said, "I volunteer you." She pointed at Carrot.

Carrot blinked and shook her head. "You can't volunteer me. I have to volunteer myself."

Mrs. Smoznak held out her hand. "Then do it."

Carrot wanted to shrink down into her seat but, remembering what her essay was about, she swallowed and stood up. Mrs. Smoznak handed her the paper.

"Fear," Carrot read. She looked up. "My essay is about fear."

Mrs. Smoznak nodded, so Carrot started to read. "The sky was the color of robins' eggs and the leaves were all golden and red, fluttering in the air. It was a perfect autumn day, a perfect day to do target practice in the woods. My uncle went off to chop wood, so I lifted my rifle and began firing at the target painted on my tin deer. I shot it once right in the center and that made me feel good. At least until the buck came. I noticed right away that he was bleeding, that he had been shot in the flank. He fell down and stood up and fell down again. It made me sick to my stomach. I looked at the part of him that wasn't wounded and pretended he was just a regular old buck, that pretty soon he would pick up his tail and leap away through the woods. But then he just fell down and stayed down. His black eyes looked at me like he was asking what I was going to do. I was so afraid, everything inside me started to shake. I was afraid to run and I was afraid to stay there. I was afraid to watch the deer die but I was more afraid that he wouldn't die. Afraid that I would have to be the one to kill him. Most of all I was afraid of death. I think I've seen

a lot of death because I used to go hunting with my"—
Carrot took a deep breath and continued—"my father and
it always scared me when he shot a deer. One second it was
alive, bounding through the woods, and the next second it
would be bleeding on the ground, still as a stone. That
scared me because I couldn't understand where it went. I
wondered if it was as scared as me. But then something
worse happened. My—my—" She blinked and looked up
from her paper.

Mrs. Smoznak was looking at her, not smiling, just listening. When Carrot looked at her, she nodded for Carrot
to go on.

Carrot took another deep breath. "My father died and I
was afraid of everything. Of people. And of never seeing
him again. And, most of all, I was afraid of death. So when
the deer fell down in front of me I was more scared than
I've ever been. I asked my father to help me. And he
answered me, right out loud. He said, 'There's nothing to
be afraid of, Carrot.' So I shot the deer. But I think he
meant other things, too. I think he meant I shouldn't be
afraid of people and loneliness. And death too." Carrot
looked up. "That's all."

She sat down. Nobody said a word. Finally, behind her,
someone started clapping. In a second everyone in the
room was applauding, even Mrs. Smoznak.

"Wow, that was better than *Moby-Dick*," someone said.

"It's so sad and so beautiful," Frannie said, patting her
on the back.

"I'm very proud of you, Carrot," Mrs. Smoznak said.
"That took a lot of courage. I think we all learned some-

thing about confronting our fears." She beamed at Carrot. "Is there anything you want to add?"

Carrot shook her head.

"Well, there's something *I* would like to add. Happy fourteenth birthday."

Everyone started clapping again. Dan leaned over and said in a loud whisper, "You're supposed to stand up and take a bow."

So she got up and bowed from the waist and she forgot all about the pink bra and her face didn't even get red.

When she got home from school she walked in the back door and saw that Babe had decorated the whole room with paper plates. They were stuck on all the walls, on the kitchen cupboards, even on the ceiling.

"Happy birthday, Carrot!" Babe yelled. "Happy birthday to you." Even though it wasn't a delivery day he was dressed as Mr. Eggs in his red bow tie and best plaid jacket. "Lookit what I did. I did all of 'em. Do you like it?" He took her by the hand and showed her every plate, explaining each drawing. "This one's Henny Penny and all the chicks. You see, 1 ran outa room. But, look—one, two, three, four." He pointed at the crayoned orange balls, reminiscent of how the chicks had looked months ago.

"Wow," Carrot said. "You did all this for me, Babe?"

"That's not all, either. We got presents too. And a birthday cake."

"Babe Turvy. That was supposed to be a surprise." Gram put her hands on her hips and looked at him in dismay.

Babe looked crestfallen so Carrot flung her arms around his neck. "You made this into the nicest birthday I could ever have, Babe. Who else would draw me two dozen pictures?"

"Just me," he said proudly. "Here, open my present." He reached on top of the mantel and brought down a wrapping-paper tube tied with a red bow. "Look inside," he said. "It's a present. I made it."

It was another picture on a big rectangle of paper, laminated in clear plastic.

"It's a place mat," he said, taking it away from her. "You see, here's me and here's you at the stand. Here's the tomatoes. Here's the corn. Here's the sun. See, we both got matching hats."

"Oh, Babe. This is the best. TURVY'S PRODUCE. Did you print that yourself?"

"Almost," he said. "And Mama put it in plastic so you can spill things on it."

After Babe's present, Gram gave her a quilt. It was the crazy quilt she had been working on when she got sick. "Because you're so crazy," she said, giving Carrot a swat on the fanny.

Her mother's present was a heavy, purple parka. "Winter will be here before you know it," she said, taking the jacket from Carrot and holding it up to her for size. "And that old jacket you insist on wearing—well, I mean, it's all right for autumn but you need something warmer for winter. And guess what, everyone? I bought this with my Rainbow money." Her eyes shone with pleasure.

"It's beautiful, Mom. I love it—especially the color."

"Well, it *is* your color," her mother pointed out, draping the matching purple ribbon around Carrot's neck.

They had venison for dinner, and biscuits and boiled potatoes and corn, frozen from the summer. Every few minutes Carrot would lift her plate and comment on the place mat. "This is so pretty I hate to cover it up."

"I'll show you how to make one. After dinner. Hey—you can make one for me." Babe clapped his hands. "We can be twins."

When Carrot was certain she couldn't eat another bite Gram came out with a Tunnel of Fudge cake, lit with four-teen candles.

"Happy birthday to you—" they started to sing. There was a knock at the door.

"Oh, bother," Gram said. "If it's not the telephone, it's the door." Susan started to get up but Gram waved her down. "Finish your singing."

As the last "you-u-u" floated over the table Gram led in Dan Durbin.

"You can't just drop a check off and run," she was saying. "You've got to stay and have some birthday cake." She handed a check to Babe. "Mrs. Durbin sends this for chopping firewood."

Babe examined the check on both sides and then got up to put it in the crock.

"Sit," Gram said to Dan. "Sit over there by Carrot. She's the birthday girl."

"I know," Dan said, grinning at Carrot.

They were eating their cake and Babe was telling them about Henny Penny sitting on a little green apple for the last two days. "What should I do, Mama? Do you think she's cracked?"

Even though Babe looked so worried everyone started to laugh. Then Dan leaned over and whispered to Carrot. "I have a present for you. It's outside."

"Huh? What is it?" she asked.

He grinned and shook his head.

"Is it okay if we go outside for a minute?" Carrot said, feeling a little foolish.

"Oh, boy." Babe stood up. "Wait till I get my jacket."

"No, Babe," Gram said. "*Carrot* was invited."

Carrot looked at Babe's disappointed face and felt terrible. Babe had spent hours decorating for her birthday. "We'll be right back, Babe," she said. "Right back."

As she was zipping up her new jacket she felt the moose staring down at her. She stepped back and looked up at him, at his black, droopy lips, his glittery little eyes, the great antlers lifted in an eternal question. She thought of all the sights those little eyes had seen, all the celebrations, all the tick-tack-toe games, all the noisy dinners. What was it, she wondered. What was the question?

She unwound the purple ribbon from her neck. "Is this it?" she whispered, holding it out. "Is this what you want?" And she flung the ribbon up in the air. The purple streamers caught in the antlers and the bow settled over the moose's right eye. Carrot grinned up at him. "So long, Moose," she said, giving a little wave. And she followed Dan out into the frosty air.

He bent and picked something out of the snow. "Happy birthday," he said, handing her a tall paper cup.

Carrot started to laugh. "A Velvet Thundercloud?"

"I kept it in the freezer for you."

"Wow," she said. "That's a weird birthday present."

"Well, I'm a pretty weird guy."

"I know," she said, laughing again.

"Hey—you want to take a walk?"

"Okay," she said, setting the Velvet Thundercloud back in the snow.

"Carrot!" Babe opened the back door and called out into the night. "Come back. You promised, Carrot. Don't forget."

But Carrot had gone too far. All she could hear was their footsteps in the snow and the sound of her own laughter.